THE MOUNTAIN FOG

K E MEUIR

Irish Viking
publishing

ISBN: 978-0-578-98219-9 (SC)
ISBN: 978-0-578-98220-5 (E)

Library of Congress Control Number: 2021918054

❀ Created with Vellum

To all the students who made me a better teacher and a better storyteller,
thank you.

ACKNOWLEDGEMENT

I sat down to write a story never thinking it would turn into a book. Along came a man whose encouragement and faith in my writing made it impossible not to finish the story. My fellow writer and best beloved, Mark David Albertson, gave this story wings where it had stone feet. For his patience in reading the transcript and his ideas for making the story come alive, I am grateful. The hours he devoted to listening to me toss around character and plot ideas made for many a lovely evening on the patio of our Texas ranch. I am indebted to him.

Thank you to Lara Kennedy for her editing skills. She was precise and helpful in so many ways.

Thank you to Irish Viking Publishing Co. for taking a chance on a debut novel.

PREFACE

A small fire flickered in the recesses of a cave high in the mountain. The flames danced and threw vague shadows against the walls of the cave. A woman sat beside the fire, hunched over a book bound in brown leather, cracked and wrinkled with age. She muttered to herself and turned the yellowed pages with impatient hands. "It's here somewhere. I know it's here somewhere," muttered the woman. Long black hair hung down her back in waves, and occasionally she reached up and brushed a stray lock out of her way.

Holding the book to the fire so that the light illuminated the words, she caught her breath. With trembling hands, she carefully turned the pages and read the words again. She sat upright and spread her hands across the words as if to honor them. Breathing deeply, she smiled—a smile of satisfaction. Everything she ever wanted was before her now with the words found on these pages. Everything she had ever craved was within her reach. Her smile grew until she threw back her head and laughed aloud.

1

THE VILLAGE

"Last one to the bell tower has to clean up after the sheep!" The slender girl with a blond braid that reached down to the middle of her back, hitched her skirts up to her knees and took off running. "No fair! You got a head start!" The small group of children darted after her; girls with skirts pulled high and young boys with bare feet that pounded the dirt path, kicking up dust as they ran towards the village green.

"Wait for me," cried a small plaintive voice. "You always leave me behind!" The smallest of the group, a pug-nosed boy with hair the color of wheat straw, put his head down and willed his small feet and legs to move faster. The girl looked over her shoulder and smiled at the boy. *He tries like mad to keep up!* She shortened her stride, letting the other children pass her, until finally the boy drew next to her. "Ean, you're getting faster every time we race. You'll see, it won't be this year, but next and you'll catch up to your brother and then pass him by. Your legs are growing faster than the rest of you can keep up with them!" She laughed as she said it, and the boy puffed out his chest and ran even faster.

Screaming with laughter, the children rounded the last bend before the bell tower. The girl kept pace with Ean until they reached the village center and fell to the grass, gulping in air like fish out of water! "Looks like you have to clean up after the sheep again, Ean!" His older brother teased the small boy.

"No, I'm afraid it's me this time. At the last moment, Ean pulled a step ahead of me. He's getting faster, Tomas. You watch out, he'll be beating you soon enough." The girl lay back and let the soft grass tickle her neck. She watched the clouds chase each across the sky in such a hurry they had no time to settle into interesting shapes but kept shifting with the overhead wind. She glanced over at the small flock of sheep, cropping the rich green grass closer than any scythe could cut it. She sighed. *It's Granny Matilda's flock. They eat faster and leave more droppings than anyone else's sheep!*

She stretched her arms overhead and sat up, brushing the grass from her skirt as she did. "I better start. The men will be bringing out the tables soon, and they will curse to the sky if they must step in sheep droppings to do it. Let's make a game of it! Celia, you grab the buckets and Dara, you get the rakes and shovels." Before long, the children were running around the green, searching for sheep pellets, crying out when they found some. The little squad of workers shoveled them into the buckets to be carried off.

In a large, stone cottage with rock walls and a newly thatched roof, a man sat down to his morning tea. "What in blazes is all that noise?" he asked, blowing on his tea to cool it. His wife set a plate of warm bread, cheese, and sausages on the table and smiled down at him, "Oh, it's the children, dear heart. They've been racing around the village all morning. I believe they've finally made it to the green."

The man left his breakfast and stepped out on the front porch. From his viewpoint, he watched the children scurrying around the green, excitedly calling out when they found a pile worth picking up. "She's got them all lined up and working, same as usual," he called over his shoulder. He shook his head and smiled to himself.

On the other side of the green, a young boy with dark hair that fell across his forehead and half covered his eyes, watched as well. He smiled when he saw how the girl had all the children running around the green with rakes, shovels, and buckets. *She's the only one I know who can make picking up after sheep an adventure.* He smiled to himself and then melted back into the shadows of the trees, calling to his dog as he did.

Two by two, groups of men began carrying out heavy trestle tables and long benches to set up in the square. Women followed with armfuls of brightly colored linen to cover the rough wood. "Dara, Celia, stop that running about and come put the cloths on the tables." The women piled the tablecloths in the middle of one of the tables and turned to watch the children with their rakes and shovels.

A tall woman with streaks of gray in her dark hair put her arm around a younger woman. "Just think, before you know it, your babe will be running with this pack of wolves we call children." She smiled at the younger woman and patted her huge belly. "Not soon enough, believe me," the young woman replied as she leaned her head against the older woman's shoulder. Together they watched Dara and Celia shake out the cloths and soon the girls had the tables dressed in the bright linens. "Ma, can we pick some flowers to put on the tables?" The girls looked hopefully at their mother. The woman smiled fondly and nodded, and the girls scurried off to rob flowers from whatever garden would yield the prettiest.

Tomas rounded up the boys, his brother Ean among them, and started giving orders; plates and bowls had to be brought out, table settings for the girls to put around, wood gathered for the bonfire later in the evening, and someone had to herd that flock of sheep out of the green and back to their pasture for the night. The green echoed with calling voices, and laughter rang out like church bells pealing on a Sunday morning.

Before the evening sun set, the villagers crowded around the tables, gossiping and comparing each other's roast mutton and new potatoes, vegetables from summer gardens, and last year's cider pressed from fall apples and stored in cold cellars for just such a celebration. They watched the children chasing and tagging each other, whirling and dodging hands that reached to grab, all the while squealing as only children who have not a care in the world can do.

After the last morsel of food had been pushed around plates and enjoyed, Ean's father, Dylan, brought out an old fiddle, and after tuning it up, began playing a mournful tune. A hush fell over the villagers, and the children stopped chasing and sat down on the grass or stood next to a parent leaning against them to listen to the soft, sweet notes. Dylan walked among the tables, playing softly and then raising the volume until he had everyone's attention. Tears gathered in the old folks' eyes, spilling over and running unnoticed down their worn cheeks. Young lovers held hands and leaned their heads towards each other.

Dylan drew the last long note with his bow and pulled the fiddle out from under his chin. Like the wind that comes up without notice, the villagers let out a long sigh as if they had been holding their breath for ages. Dylan smiled at them, and then drawing his bow against the strings once more said, "Enough of all that. Let's have some music we can dance to!" And dance they did, until poor Dylan begged to go home and put away his fiddle until next time.

Slowly, two by two, couples called to their children and called out their good nights. Stars twinkled overhead and the moon smiled down on them as they walked slowly home.

2

A CHANGE

The man stepped out on his front porch with a steaming cup of tea he held in both his hands. He leaned against one of the upright posts and gazed across at the empty green. The village was silent now, but he could still hear the children's laughter, their voices raised as they called out to one another. He could see the slim shapes of the children running around like mad, cleaning up sheep droppings, and making a game of it. He could hear the fiddle music in his mind, though there had been no music for the longest time. No feasts, no music, no gosipping women carrying heavy platters of roasted meat and vegetables to the tables, no men swinging a crossed leg back and forth in comfort while they drew on pipes filled with sweet smelling tobacco. The green was silent now. The children, the ones who were left, were all hidden behind closed doors.

The man finished the last of his tea and thought about all the changes that had come to his beloved village. Running a hand through his hair, he took one last look at the green before turning into his cottage.

Every two years, the villagers elected a mayor who served as the head of the committee and chief constable. For the past few years, they'd been content to select the same man, Erik Tamen, an oversized man with thunder in his voice and a laugh that echoed throughout the valley. Usually, one of the happiest men in the village, Erik could be fierce when called upon to roust the occasional traveling drunkard or help defend a herd of sheep from wolves. Tall and stout as an oak, Erik was easy to spy with his bright red hair and bristling beard. It was his habit to stride through town every evening, calling out to his neighbors, sharing a joke or a story. He kept the peace, reassuring the villagers that their life would continue as it always had, quiet and comfortable.

Recently, a change had come over the village. Now the villagers crept silently about their work, looking over their shoulders nervously. The joyful sound of children's laughter no longer floated across the clear air. Most frequently heard were the sharp tones of parents scolding their children and calling anxiously for them, hastening them inside the cottages. As soon as the sun set, the villagers shut each cottage door and barred the windows. Not a soul crossed the village square once the evening shadows lengthened.

Before blowing out the lanterns and snuffing the candles, the parents snugged their children into their beds and set guards to block the bedroom doors. They melted wax to pour into cracks and crevices in the walls to seal them tight. They stuffed rags around the doors and windows. They built the fires high and watched the smoke pour up the chimneys, and they boldly sat upright, holding pitchforks, kitchen knives, any weapon they had at the ready.

Despite this caution, down from the mountain, a cold winter fog crept on silent feet, wrapping itself around trees, sliding across the canyons, and slipping like a thief into the village. The fog drifted across the village square with a calm and deadly purpose, until it surrounded one tiny cottage. Inside the cottage huddled a mother and father; the mother cradled a young girl in her arms, while the father kept watch over them both. The fog did not hesitate but relentlessly probed each corner of the cottage, searching for a way inside. Determined, it pressed each wall until it found what it was looking for, a tiny crack in the corner. Silently, the fog poured itself through the crack until it lay flat and soft on the cottage floor.

The mother's head drooped low in sleep, and the father leaned against the wall. The fog slowly, carefully crept toward the sleeping child and wrapped its cold, clammy arms around her. It lifted the child from her mother's arms, and as it did, the child became as the fog, wisps of vapor disappearing through the crack, across the village square, and high up into the mountains.

The next morning, the mother's cries and the curses of the father woke the villagers, who rushed to the cottage to aid and comfort the grieving parents. Thus, it went on and on, children disappearing no matter how vigilant the people were, no matter what precautions they took. As time passed and more children disappeared, a deep gloom settled over the village, and the people began to eye one another with suspicion and doubt. Life changed for the small village, and no more did song and laughter ring out across the valley.

3

ANOTHER CHILD

Erik Tamen woke suddenly from a deep and comfortable sleep. He lay still for a moment, wondering what had disturbed him from his slumber. It took only a moment to recognize the sounds of grieving parents. He threw back the quilt and stumbled across the dark room for his clothes hanging on the pegs.

"What is it?" mumbled his wife, still burrowed under the quilts.

"Nothing. Go back to sleep. I just heard something, and I'm going to go see what it is."

She raised her head from the pillow and listened for a moment. "I'll put water on for tea. Let me know what I can do."

He looked at his Guinevere fondly from across the room as he struggled into his clothes. No matter what happened, he could depend on her quiet strength; nothing rattled her or gave her reason to be anything but quiet and calm. It was what he loved best about her. He might rant and rave, curse the heavens, or bellow in rage against the unknown, but Guin could always calm him with a soothing hand on his shoulder or a look from her brown eyes. No children of her own brightened the small cottage, despite prayers to the gods. Once she had held a wee one in her arms, smiled down on him, and thanked the heavens for giving her a son, but that was years ago, and fate had not been kind to either Guin or her small son.

Now she mothered the children of the village freely and with no regret. They all knew that she would wipe away their tears with the hem of her skirt or the handkerchief she kept tucked into her sleeve. She bandaged the skinned knees of young boys and braided long hair as girls sat at her feet. Young hearts could pour out their worries to Guin with no fear of reprisals or judgment, so it soon became the habit for young girls to seek her advice when young men came calling. The young men also sat with Guin and discovered through her wisdom what young girls' hearts needed.

When Erik arrived at the cottage, it was surrounded by neighbors twisting their hands and muttering among themselves. As Erik strode through the small crowd and entered the cottage, he was met with a scene that he had seen now a dozen times: the weeping mother collapsed near the fire as her relatives tried in vain to soothe her; the father, numb with disbelief, repeating over and over the same words, "We sat with her. We held Celia in our arms."

The father looked up when Erik entered, anguish written across his face. Erik rested a hand on his shoulder, but the man appeared not to notice.

"I have no words to help you, John. Except to say I'm sorry."

John looked up from his seat. "Don't give me words, Erik. Find her, find our Celia and our Dara. You're our mayor, our constable. It's your job to keep us safe, keep our children safe. No more words, Erik. Find our children and bring them back to us. The only words that I want to hear is that you have found them."

From across the village square, a determined couple marched to join the crowd outside the cottage. The man had a scowl on his face, and his wife strode behind him, pushing him forward with a hand tight on his shoulder.

"Another one, Mayor?" said the man with a sneer. "How many now, Mayor?" The word *mayor* was emphasized and made to sound more like a curse than an honorific.

The woman behind him crossed her arms and looked around at

her neighbors. "Why do you put up with this?" she asked. "Why do you let him say the same thing over and over but do nothing?"

"Please, not now, Sean. This is not the time for blame. Give comfort if you can, and if you can't, then go back home and leave us alone."

"Wouldn't you like that, Erik? If we all just pretended that you were doing the right thing, when in fact you're as helpless as the rest of us. We elected you mayor and constable to keep this village safe, and right now you're doing a pretty poor job of it, I'd say."

His words reached the ears of all those present, and the grumbling and mutters increased, as well as the dark looks sent in Erik's direction.

As Erik made his way back to his cottage, he considered what John and Sean had said. It was his job; the people had elected him, they trusted him. His duty was clear, but the way to accomplish it slipped away from him like a fish in water. When the children first began disappearing, he had questioned every villager, searched every home and barn. He had walked across every field and through the forests but found no trace of any of them. How, then, could he find them now? Looking back on it, he realized that he had fallen into a pattern of comforting the villagers and little else. He didn't blame them for their dark looks, their muttering as he walked by, for what had he done to help them? His broad shoulders slumped as he walked back through his own door.

Erik and Guin shared a large, stone cottage, whitewashed, with a newly thatched roof. Before he'd brought Guin here as a young bride, his hands had lovingly laid each stone with mortar between to hold them strong and fast. His chimney was straight and drew smoke from the huge fireplace below. A wide porch with rocking chairs greeted company when they mounted the steps to visit. Inside, the cottage was warm and snug, with a fire burning brightly in the main room. A large kitchen to the right of the fireplace held a long table and cupboards and plenty of shelves. Most of the shelves carried the cooking essentials—flour, sugar, and tea—but some of them held bright blue-and-white dishes and vases. To the left of the fireplace was the main sitting room, with benches and chairs crafted by Erik and dressed with cushions Guin had sewn to give comfort at the end of the day. A hallway ran off the main room to a bedroom, and above everything was a loft with several beds. Erik had built each bed himself out of timber harvested from the forest behind the village, thinking that someday children would race up and down the ladder to the loft and the sounds of laughter would echo down until he or Guin shushed them all for the night. Instead, the loft lay empty and still.

"Another one, my love?" asked Guin anxiously.

"Yes, Celia this time. It means they have lost both their girls! May all the devils take the creature who torments us so! I can't keep searching the same places over and over. There has to be more that I can do!"

She placed a steaming cup of tea in front of him and sat down across the table. "It's past time you talked with Granny. You know it, and I know it. No more thinking you can solve this on your own."

"No!" Erik slammed his hand on the table, rattling the cups of tea. "By all the fates, you know I won't. I haven't forgotten what she did, Guin. I can never forget!"

Guin reached her hand across the table and laid it gently on Erik's. The very touch settled him, as it always did. His anger turned to sorrow, but he was determined.

"Erik, you know that Granny wasn't the cause; she only had the telling of it. She didn't cause our Matthew to be taken from us; she only meant to warn us. There was nothing she could do, nothing we could do. I don't ask you to forgive her, Erik, but there are more children gone than just our boy. It's time to put aside your anger and seek her guidance. She might have a telling about this that will help. I know you are no fool, to put your pride before the answers you need."

His pain shone in his eyes, and tears brimmed over to run down his cheeks into his beard. He gripped his cup between his hands and nodded. He would see if Granny had answers for his village.

4
FRIENDS

Two small figures stood at the back of the crowd; a boy with dark hair that fell across his forehead into his eyes, and a girl with a blond braid that fell halfway down her back. She reached out to find his hand as they listened to the sounds of grief.

"Let's go. We can't do anything here." Conor pulled his hand away and walked across the road to a path that led between the houses toward the fields beyond the village. He kicked up dust with his bare feet as he increased his speed, to get away from the sounds behind him. His face was locked in a fierce scowl, and he didn't stop until he reached the copse of giant oaks on the far side of the field. He threw himself on the ground and wrapped his arms around a small brown dog, burying his face in its scruff.

Concobhar had been on his own for years, with only the small dog he called Wolf. He'd once had a family, parents who must have loved him, though he couldn't be sure, because memory failed him. He couldn't picture them in his mind, nor remember a single touch or word from them. All he knew was that one day, they were both gone from him. The villagers had guessed that, like gypsies, they had taken to wandering, but no one could understand leaving the boy behind. They had tried to take him into their homes and care for him, but he wouldn't have it. They would wake up to find him gone, back to a tiny cottage at the edge of the village that he'd claimed for his own.

After so many attempts at rescuing him, Erik Tamen had persuaded the villagers to leave him be and let him stay where he was most comfortable. They provided food for the boy until he was able to grow or catch his own. They dropped by with cast-off clothes, mostly too big, as the boy was small and scrawny.

He took to roaming the fields and forests that ringed the village. He learned to identify the plants and birds that he found there. He could lie for hours and watch a caterpillar crawl across the fallen leaves or a hawk wheel and whistle above his head. He raised himself, looked after himself, and spent most of his time by himself, happy with his own company. The fields and forests were his refuge. "I'd rather talk with a creature than people," he said, and he meant it, though most people didn't understand his need for solitude. Years of time on his own had become a habit, one that was hard to break.

It was a young girl named Tilly who carved a hole in the wall that he had built around himself. She did it not with a hammer or chisel, but with a steadfast belief that he needed her company, no matter how fiercely he glared at her. Named for her great-grandmother, Matilda, Tilly was as bright as Conor was dark. Her long blonde hair was pulled into a braid that fell down her back, often with bits of straw or grass clinging to it. Her blue eyes laughed at him—and with him, on the rare occasions she could get him to laugh. Her face seemed to be split in two with a smile that showed her cheerful nature, a love for anyone and anything, but mostly for Conor. She recognized the need he had deep inside him for something he couldn't put into words, and she determined that she would be the one to fulfill it for him.

They soon became a common sight around the village, running, chasing, exploring, or sometimes talking quietly. The villagers shook their heads in amazement that this unlikely pair would form such a bond, but they soon came to accept it as natural and knew that if they were to see one, they were likely to find the other close behind. Tilly had a way of taking Conor's hand and pulling him along on her adventures that, despite his initial unwillingness to participate, was impossible to resist, until soon he no longer tried.

"You worry too much, Conor," she laughed at him time and again.

"Well, you don't worry enough. You drag me off to the most ridiculous places, caves and creeks and far-off fields. You know, as much as I like the animals, there are some that we should worry about!"

"I'll tell you what—you worry too much; I worry not enough. They should throw us into a pot and stir us together, and we would worry just right."

"There's no logic to that," he grumbled. "It doesn't make a bit of sense to me. And it wouldn't make sense to anyone else either. Tilly, you have to make sense once in a while." She laughed and ran off, and he followed, like he always did.

Today, Tilly was as solemn as Conor as she settled down next to him in the shade of the trees. She absentmindedly stroked Wolf's fur, her mind on the scene in the village. "How many does this make now?" she asked.

"Eight. Eight children stolen right from under their parents' noses. Inside their houses, behind locked doors." Conor said it all through clenched teeth. "And no one knows where they are or how they've been taken."

Tilly sat on the grass and drew her knees up until she could rest her chin on them. Tears streamed down her face, wetting her skirt. "Celia, this time. My sweet, sweet Celia. She never hurt anyone or anything. First Dara, and now Celia. What will they do? How will they survive without their girls?"

Conor shook his head and scooted close enough to put his arm around her shoulder. She leaned her head against him and gulped back her tears. Sitting up straight, she used the hem of her skirt to wipe away her tears and dry her face.

"Have you noticed anything about the children?" she asked.

"What do you mean?"

"Think about it. At first, they were small babes, but Dara was nine and Celia was twelve. Not much younger than we are."

"I didn't think about it, but you're right. Is that important, do you think?" His scowl deepened.

"I don't know. Just thinking out loud, I guess. Do you ever think that it could be us?"

"No, I don't. I can't think about that." He sighed and lay back on the grass, Wolf beside him.

"Why did you name him Wolf? Hate to tell you this, but he is not very wolflike, you know."

"No, but he's his own dog, and he might just decide to up and leave me someday, just like a wolf. That's as good a name as I'm willing to give him until I know he's going to stay with me," Conor said fondly as he stroked the dog's coat.

No one really remembered when Wolf had appeared or when he took up with Conor, least of all Conor himself. It seemed like he was there one day and had never left. He wasn't much to look at, despite his grand name, being small with brown, wiry hair. His ears stood straight up until the tips fell over, and his tail looked as if it really needed a few more inches to be complete.

The little dog could run like a streak, flat out, with a grin on his face that told the story of the happiness in his heart. He didn't bark much, sometimes when they ran and played together, but never when he was on guard. On the occasion when he perceived a threat to Conor or Tilly, a deep growl would start down low in his chest, a growl that felt like it should have come from a much bigger dog. Despite his small stature, that growl persuaded most would-be threats to back away quietly.

Wolf always slept in Conor's small house, keeping guard throughout the night. It occurred to Conor that Tilly should take Wolf home with her at night, but her mother wouldn't hear of it. "No mangy cur is sleeping in this house, bringing fleas and who knows what into my clean house," her mother declared. Conor had just shrugged.

5

MATILDA

Granny Matilda stepped out of her small cottage and, shading her eyes against the glare of the sun, stared at the ridge of mountains in the distance, although she knew she wouldn't see anything more than she had seen yesterday or the day before. Despite not seeing anything with her eyes, Granny began to have a sense of what was there, so high in the mountains that it was hidden behind the clouds. She watched now as Erik Tamen came striding down the lane toward her house.

"Hmmm. I thought I was wrong and that he wasn't going to come after all," she muttered under her breath. She backed through the door to put water on for tea. Erik stopped at her gate, waiting for an invitation to enter. He knew better than to come into Granny's small space without an invitation. Too many souls had been chased away with the tongue lashing of their life when they thought their need to enter was greater than her need to be alone.

"Well, don't just stand there like a dolt. Come in and sit and have some tea with me, Erik Tamen," she said through the door-way. "I'll bring it out and we can sit in the sunshine. I need some sun to warm my bones this morning, and the view is good to look at."

He settled down on a wicker chair and accepted the proffered cup of tea.

"What brings you to my door?" she asked.

"Another child has gone missing in the night. It makes eight now, Granny. I have no idea what to do, but Guin says I need to come to you. What do you know of this, Granny Matilda?"

Granny didn't answer, just stared toward the mountains. Erik began to fidget, thinking her hearing was going, along with everything else. "Did you hear me?" he asked.

Still no answer from Granny. Instead, she asked, "Have you noticed anything different about the mountains lately, Erik Tamen?"

"The mountains?" His tone belied his confusion.

"Yes, look. Have you noticed anything different about them?"

He glanced toward the mountains. "No, they're the same blasted mountains that I've been seeing since I was in short pants, Granny. They haven't changed. They're just there, always."

"No, Erik Tamen. Look at them with me. Really look. What do you see?"

Erik looked toward the mountains, and he did notice something, something unusual. There were black clouds—huge, towering black clouds, swirling in constant motion around the highest peak. Had they looked like this before? Why hadn't he noticed?

"You see it, don't you, Erik Tamen?" asked Granny.

"What in the devil's name is that? I've never seen those black clouds before. What does it mean?"

Granny didn't answer right away. She continued to stare at the mountains and sip her tea.

Granny had been born Matilda so many years before that even she had lost track of her age. She was Tilly's great-grandmother, Tilly's namesake. Over the years, she had watched her village prosper; watched children grow into strong adults, marry and raise their own young babes.

Granny Matilda knew things without seeing or hearing them. She had long since given up trying to explain her abilities. She accepted it as her gift and her curse: a gift when the knowledge she possessed was helpful or accepted as wisdom, a curse when what she knew to be true frightened her friends. As time passed, she learned to keep her counsel when warnings of coming events were not welcome. No one wanted to know that crops were going to fail because a hailstorm would pound them into the ground. No one wanted to know the day and the hour of their death, even though it might give them a chance to put their house in order. She gladly shared the telling of a new healthy baby or the coming rains when the farmers squinted anxiously at the sky, but the bad news, she'd learned to keep to herself.

She'd seen this latest tragedy coming, although even she did not understand or realize the reasons for it. She knew that there was a new and ominous presence on the mountain, a presence that hungered for what it could not have without stealing. When the children began to disappear, she tried to tell herself that it was wild animals that had stolen the children, but she continued to look toward the mountain, and she wondered.

For many nights, she'd stood vigil at her window, listening but mostly watching with her inner eye. Yet night after night, she came up with nothing. It was only on a moonstruck night that she could see in her mind the fog creeping down the mountainside, approaching the village with cold purpose. A deep and abiding chill struck her, and she left the window and crawled beneath her covers to lie there, shivering. "I am too old for this," she muttered. "They cannot expect me to help them after all these years."

The next day, she'd sat in her chair in the sun and closed her eyes. She'd set her mind to wandering in the mountains, searching for answers. She passed the Mountain Folk, who dwelled in the caves halfway up the mountains, when she realized they had no answers for her. She continued to climb the mountain in her mind, noticing that as she went higher, there were no sounds. No birds sang, no insects hummed, no leaves or grass rustled as creatures crept through them. Only silence, a silence so thick as to be impenetrable.

Finally, she reached the top of the mountain, where the black clouds swirled without ever stopping. There she found a cave, and she knew without entering that an evil like none she had ever beheld lived within its depths. In her mind, she stood outside the cave and listened and watched. Almost immediately, she realized that she had been discovered. Whoever was in there knew she was outside. How could that be? She traveled only in her mind, but in her mind, she heard a sound, a sound that raised the hairs on the back of her neck even as she sat in the warm sunshine.

Come in, come in, she heard, though it was not a voice she heard with her ears, only in her mind. It was a whisper, like the dry leaves that blow in the cold wind. Quickly, she pulled back from the cave and returned to her small dwelling, with its comfortable chair. She leaned back in that chair, gasping for breath, willing her heart to stop its racing beats.

Now, as she sat in the autumn sunshine with Erik Tamen, she remembered the cold knowledge that had filled her that day, knowledge that was almost too much to bear.

"Erik Tamen, I believe that is where our children now dwell. At the top of that mountain, among those clouds that are never still and yet never blow away. I believe our children were taken there by a force that I don't recognize, a force I don't know how to fight. I don't know if they are there willingly or against their wishes. I don't know for what purpose they are there, but this I know; they are there, and the only way to bring them home is to climb that mountain."

Erik Tamen dropped his gaze from the mountaintop and fixed it on Granny Matilda. He fought to slow his breathing and hold his tongue. His thoughts, however, raced as the deer from the hunter. He thought of Granny's warning that his first and only child would not see the end of his first winter. He remembered his anger toward her, as if she had caused his death by the telling of it. His hands again clenched, as they had years ago, when his dear Guin had held him back from storming out of their home and seeking her out. The same heaviness sat on his chest now. How did Granny know these things? Was she somehow to blame? Yet there was not a doubt in his mind that her words were true. He cursed her under his breath and let the words carry away his fierce anger.

Granny met his anger with a steady look from eyes that never wavered. She felt the heaviness in his heart, but also his determination. He pushed himself up from the chair and stood over her.

"Then climb that blasted mountain I will!" he thundered. "I will bring our children back where they belong." He stepped off her porch and headed away without a backward look.

"Erik Tamen! Wait! You have no idea of the danger, of the force that I've felt up there. You can't understand what is there; you have no idea how to combat it. You can't just storm off without knowing!"

Her words stopped him as though she had reached out her hands to him. He turned slowly and faced her. "You know how to go there, don't you? You know how to see the children? You have that power, don't you?"

She nodded slowly.

"Then do it! Go there and find out what you can. I give you until tomorrow to find the knowledge that will help me bring our children home. It lies with you, Granny Matilda, to use your powers to help me. I will heed your counsel, but mark me, Granny, I will not wait past the morrow." With these words, he left her.

Granny sighed deeply, and despite her brave heart, she felt a fear deep within her that she could not shake. She settled herself in her chair and set her mind loose to climb the mountain once again. As her mind wandered up the steep sides and her hands relaxed, her teacup rolled across the floor, unseen, unheard. Deeper and deeper, she retreated into her mind, as higher and higher she climbed. Once more, she stood outside the cave entrance and listened with all her might. No sound emanated from the cave, only a cold breeze that brushed past her as if it, too, wanted to escape the depths.

Taking a deep breath, Granny stepped inside, letting the cold wrap itself around her, drawing her into the dark that the outside light could not penetrate. As her eyes adjusted, she saw that a dim light faintly illuminated the dark some distance from the entrance. Gripping her woolen skirt with both hands, Granny made her way toward the light.

"Make yourself small," she whispered to herself. "Make yourself silent." *Small and silent,* she repeated over and over as she crept toward the light.

As she neared the source of the light, she saw shapes covered in dark cloth, laid out one after another, dozens of them. No sound came from the shapes, no movement, save a slight, almost imperceptible rhythmic rising and falling of the cloth. She stared until her eyes burned but could see nothing more than that slight shift in the cloth. No hand, no foot emerged, and yet she knew, without a doubt, that before her were the children. Scores of them—many more than just her village had given up. She held her breath, even as her heart began to drum inside her chest. Still, she stayed in the shadows, knowing that there was much more she needed to know to help Erik Tamen. Why were the children here? Were they sleeping? If so, it seemed almost the sleep of the dead. A figure glided from the back of the cave, moving among the silent figures on the stone platforms. "Oh, little ones. How you sleep, how you do sleep! Soon it will be time for you to wake and do your master's bidding. Not yet. Be patient, little ones. Soon, very soon!"

Granny watched the figure move from one distant shape to another: bending here, straightening a cloth there, whispering all the time. As the figure glided ever closer, Granny sensed a familiarity in it, a recognition of the voice. Rooted to the spot as if her feet were the very stone she stood on, Granny watched helplessly as the figure moved closer, became clearer in the faded light. The figure stopped some distance from Granny and, straightening, looked Granny in the eyes.

A chuckle first and then an outright laugh echoed throughout the chamber. "So you've come back, Granny Matilda! I've been expecting you. *We've* been expecting you!" The figure took a step toward her and held out a hand to Granny. "You are surprised to see me." What should have been a question was stated as a fact.

Granny stared, disbelieving what her eyes and mind refused to allow. This could not be. This woman who had left their village years ago, leaving her son behind to fend for himself, now stood before her with a cold smile and piercing eyes. Her long, black hair cascaded across her shoulders and down her back in waves. Dressed in the plainest of robes, she wore them like a queen, sweeping the hem along the floor as she stepped ever closer to Granny. Her outstretched hand was regal, and her voice carried the weight of command in it. "Come. Come and see your lost children," she commanded.

Without knowing how and or why, Granny's feet moved as if they obeyed only the figure before them. The woman reached for Granny's hand, sending cold chills up her arm.

"See for yourself, Granny Matilda. Oh, I do remember you. How I remember you! You with the gift of sight. I know this is not really you standing before me, but it will do for now. Until we meet in body, Granny, this will do just fine. See these little ones. They slumber, but not for long. When the time is right, we will rouse them and create an army with no equal. Without fear, without a soul, these little soldiers will do our bidding with no question. An army of innocents, Granny. Think of it! There can be no more powerful army than that!"

Granny pulled her hand away from the grip that bound her. Taking a step back, she shook her head. "You cannot do this to these children. We won't allow it!"

Peals of laughter answered her protests. "You cannot stop it. There is nothing you can do to stop it, not you or anyone!"

The laughter chased Granny as she retreated from the cave and fled down the mountain to the safety of her cottage and the warm sunshine that eased the aches in her body but could not ease the ache in her heart as she sat in her chair in the sun. She took a deep breath and sat still, remembering the laughter, the voice, and the woman who spoke the hated words.

"Our poor children, our poor, poor children." Tears trickled down her worn face and fell without notice onto her lap.

"Granny, Granny! Wake up, Granny." Tilly shook her shoulder softly. "Are you awake?"

Granny started in her rocking chair and gazed up into Tilly's face. "The sun was so warm, and I was so tired. I fell asleep. Silly old fool, sleeping in the middle of the day on my own porch." Granny stooped to pick up her forgotten teacup and headed into the cottage with Tilly, Conor, and Wolf on her heels.

Tilly laughed and hugged Granny close. "You are not any kind of fool, especially not an old one. You have more energy than all of us, save maybe Wolf. He never stops moving."

"Except when he's sleeping, which seems to be a good part of the day anymore," Conor muttered, giving Wolf a look as the pup curled up in front of the fireplace.

"Do this old woman a service, Conor, please? You and Wolf go bring in my sheep. I am too tired to make the climb up the hill to the back pasture. You'll find them there."

"Wolf, let's go get sheep." The dog sprang up from his spot and followed Conor out the door.

"Granny, are you feeling all right? I've not known you to give over bringing in the sheep at any time." The concern on Tilly's face erased her usual smile.

"Sit, girl. I'm fine. I wanted a chance to talk with you alone. I am well, but I am worried. Sit and listen to me now." Granny gripped Tilly's hands in both hers, pulling her toward her. "You and Conor have been friends for years. You've grown up together, though you have not completed that journey. I have watched you all these past years, you and Conor, and I delight in your friendship. Tilly, my only love, there are hard times coming for our village and for you both, most especially Conor. I see in him great things, things that he has no idea of within him, but I know that there are forces that will try him as nothing on this earth could do."

"You frighten me, Granny. Why do you do this? What exactly are you trying to warn me of? I wish you would speak plainly, not in riddles that my poor brain can't unravel."

"You know that I can see things, things that will happen in the future, things that have happened in the past, that are hidden from most of us? You know this, you believe this?"

"Yes, I know that you have the gift of sight. You have seen something about Conor, haven't you? Is he in danger? Is he the next child who will go missing?" Her eyes pleaded with Granny to tell her the truth, as difficult as it might be to hear.

"No, no." Granny waved her hand. "He will not go missing, but he will be tested, and I fear for him. I have seen that he is capable of great things, things that no one of us can even imagine. I think the test that he will face might be more than he can bear, and he will need you to guide him, to help him. Tilly, you must not doubt him, even when it looks as if he has turned his back on everything that you love. If he loses you or your love, it will be the end of him. Please, promise me that no matter what happens, you will have faith in Conor."

"Granny, you frighten me, but yes, I promise. He is my friend, my only friend. I cannot think of turning away from him for any reason."

"I'm sorry to frighten you. It is not my intention, sweet girl." Her eyes lost their steely glint, and her hands on Tilly's relaxed as she sat back in her chair. "It is sometimes a curse to know more than I should." She sighed and closed her eyes again, and her voice drifted into a soft whisper. "He has such greatness in him, greatness that I had no idea of before I saw the things that I did. The danger he faces will test not only him, but you as well, and I am so afraid that he won't be ready to face these things. You either, for that matter, my love."

"Granny, does this have anything to do with our missing children?"

"Yes, my love, but I'm not sure how. Sometimes when I see things, the picture is not complete. It is sometimes just a sense, but a strong one. At any rate, I don't understand how you have anything to do with it. Erik Tamen is going to try to find them, and I wish him well. He will need all the good wishes we can bestow upon him for this undertaking."

The door to the cottage banged open, and Wolf and Conor blew in with the evening wind. "The sheep are back, Granny, safe and sound. All twenty-three of them."

"Twenty-three, Concobhar! You know perfectly well that I have twenty-five woolies to my name. Where are my missing two?"

He bent down to kiss the top of her head. "Ahh, I'm teasing you, Granny. They're all in the shed, bedded and counted. I'm sorry to start you so." His eyes twinkled as he winked at Tilly. "You seem so serious, the two of you. What has got you so solemn?"

"The children, Conor, the missing children. I can't seem to think of much else."

"That reminds me. Tilly, will you take Wolf home with you tonight? I know you will have to sneak him past your mother, but I'd feel better knowing he was with you. I don't need him with me, and he's good company, though he does smell like three-day-old fish, don't you, boy?" Conor reached down and scratched Wolf's ears fondly.

She smiled her agreement. "Are you sure, Conor? Who will keep you warm in that drafty little cottage of yours without Wolf?"

"You both make sure your windows are closed tight and sealed before you sleep. I love you both."

They embraced Granny and stepped out into the fading light. Walking through the shadows in the lane, Conor took Tilly's hand in his, stopping to turn her toward him.

"Make sure you keep Wolf with you in your room tonight, promise?"

"Oh, Concobhar, you worry too much. I will see you in the morn."

"Tilly, I mean it! Wolf, go with her, and don't leave her alone for a minute." Wolf obediently trotted behind Tilly, down the lane and around the corner, until they were both lost to Conor's sight.

Sighing, Conor walked slowly to his small cottage and stepped up on the porch, which he had rebuilt himself over the summer. The boards were not as straight as he wished, and there were gaps between them bigger than there should have been, yet it was sturdy and solid, wide enough for two rough wooden chairs to sit facing the mountains. The same mountains that Granny had been facing when they stopped to see her. *What is it about those mountains?* he wondered. *There is something odd about them.*

He sat and absently reached down to scratch Wolf behind the ears, smiling when he remembered that tonight, and for as many nights as he could persuade her, the dog would be sleeping by Tilly's bedside.

"I'll miss you, but I feel better knowing you're with Tilly tonight." Conor yawned and stretched his thin frame as far as it would reach. Taking one final look at the mountain in the last of the day's light, Conor turned to enter his cottage.

His was a meager home, with few belongings and nothing really to call it a home; a wood-frame bed, a single table with two chairs in front of a fireplace made of rough stone, a pile of blankets folded neatly on the floor for Wolf, and a washstand with a basin and pitcher made up most of the furnishings. Not a picture on the walls, not a cheery vase full of flowers on the table; only a rough box with a few cooking utensils and a blackened pot hanging over the fireplace completed the single room. Conor had claimed the empty cottage after his abandonment, sweeping out the cobwebs, hauling in the meager furniture from neighbors and villagers, and making a home for himself and later Wolf when he came into Conor's life. He was not a person who needed much in the way of comforts. He'd never had them, so he never really missed them. Independence was far more important to him—that and the comfort he received from his friendship with Tilly and his companionship with Wolf. Without those two friends, life would have been far harder for Conor.

He fixed his dinner, stewed rabbit, with the carrots and potatoes he grew behind the cottage. Hanging the pot over the fire, he sat at the table, thinking of Granny Matilda and the missing children. The rich smell of the bubbling stew brought him out of his reverie. Shaking his head, he dug around in his box for a bowl and spoon, both carved from wood by his own hands. The stew was one of the best he had ever made, thanks to Granny for the herbs she generously shared with him.

Next summer, I'll grow my own herbs and expand the garden a bit. Maybe grow some berries next time. Tilly would like that, I think. He settled down with his bowl of stew, watching as darkness descended like a curtain being drawn.

6

SEAN

While Conor enjoyed dinner in front of his cozy fire, across the village, a different sort of cottage sat back from the lane amid weeds and tangles of brambles. A passerby standing in the lane looking directly at the cottage would have been forgiven for rubbing his eyes and squinting just so, for the cottage had the appearance of sitting slightly off-balance, crooked on its foundation. Made of stone and rough boards, it leaned away from the prevailing wind, as if it were too weak to stand up straight. Chinks of light escaped between the boards where someone had forgotten to fill them with good clay and mud to protect the warmth and keep out the cold night air. The chimney billowed smoke from its sides as much as from its top, giving the appearance of it being on fire. The front door, rough-hewn and without a good handle, could not close completely, leaving still more gaps for light and warm air to escape. There was no front porch to sit on, just rough steps up to the door completed the sight. There was no garden in front or back; no place to sit under the spreading branches of a tree and take one's ease graced this place. Mean and stingy, it mirrored well the two who lived in it.

Inside, the cottage was as rough as Conor's but somehow lacked the warmth that his held. A cloud of smoke from the fireplace hung above the heads of the two people sitting at the rough board table. Bowls of greasy stew sat in front of them, and the man stirred his over and over, searching unsuccessfully for bits of meat among the turnips and potatoes.

Sean McCullogh squinted at his wife, Doireann, through the haze. Sean was a thin man, with wispy, mouse-brown hair that he combed over his pate with his fingers in hopes of covering the baldness. He had the look of a man who is never satisfied with his life. "Is this the best we have for dinner, woman? This doesn't look fit for any man."

"And when was the last time you brought any meat to this home for me to cook with? When was the last time you brought anything worth having into this house, I might ask?" Her voice was sullen, her face screwed up into a frown that never seemed to leave it. Doireann was as heavy as he was thin, but while she should have looked plump and jolly, her girth instead made her seem threatening. Her eyes were lost in the folds of fat on her face, and her hair hung in lank strands down to her shoulders. The only time her eyes showed any glint of good humor was when a bit of gossip was coming her way or she was passing on some story, true or not, to the other villagers. Everyone in the village knew that if there was a story that needed relating, hand it to Doireann, and it would be spread across the village before the church bells rang on Sunday.

He sighed and raised the spoon to his mouth. Determined to avoid another argument, one he was sure to lose, like all the others over the years, he changed the subject quickly. "What do you hear in the village today?"

She sat back in her chair with a look of satisfaction on her face. "You know another child went missing in the night," she purred. "And Erik Tamen, as usual, knows nothing about it and has no idea how to stop it. The people are getting mighty fed up with him, I think. I heard a lot of grumbling today. There was quiet talk among the folks that maybe he just isn't up to the job. Perhaps he's good enough to keep our sheep safe, but not our children. There was even some talk about looking around for a replacement. Oh yes, I heard a lot of grumbling today!"

And you probably added to it, he thought to himself.

"I tell you, Sean, they won't put up with this much longer. I hear he went to Granny for help. I never thought I'd see the day he would go to that old witch for anything. That's the measure of his desperation, I think. You mark my words; the people won't be keeping him on as constable and mayor. They'll be looking for someone to take his place, someone with answers. This will be your chance to step forward, you know. I expect if you could come up with a plan, the people would be more than willing to listen to you."

While it should have sounded like encouragement, her words nagged at him, as they had for the past dozen years of their marriage. He knew keenly how disappointed she was in him and their life together. Looking around, he couldn't say he blamed her. *I could have done better by her, but she hasn't always been the best helpmate either.* "And what answers do you suppose I can come up with, woman? Erik has looked high and low for the children, there have been no strangers in our village for months, and yet we keep losing children every week." His voice reflected his frustration.

"I never said you had to solve it, you dimwit, just come up with a reasonable-sounding plan. The villagers will be happy with any plan that sounds reasonable, and you could take your rightful place as a man of respect. We could get out of this miserable hut you call a cottage and into something finer. I could wear good woolen dresses and maybe have a bit of lace at the collar and sleeves. And instead of that bowl of broth and turnips, you could dine on roast lamb and vegetables."

Sean sighed and looked down at the table. *If only it were that easy,* he thought to himself. *Come up with a plan and overnight be elevated to a place of respect and ease. But wait, at some point, you might have to put that plan into action and get results. What then? What happens when it becomes clear that your plan has no backbone to it and is as spineless as the man who put it forth? There goes the fine life, good food, and dresses with lace. We'll be lucky if they don't drive us away from the village and we end up living in the forest. What will become of us then?*

"I'll think on it, Doireann, I really will. And if I come up with something, I'll talk with you about it. Maybe you could help me think of a way to help."

"Aye, aye," she muttered. Grabbing up his bowl, she headed to the corner of the cottage set aside for a rough kitchen. *He'll think about it. Think, think, think is all he does. No action from this one, ever.* She banged the bowl into a basin of greasy water and set to scrubbing it half-heartedly.

Another sigh from Sean as he searched in his pocket for his pipe and a pinch of tobacco. The only solace he took in the evening was his bowl full of tobacco and a bit of quiet from his wife. If only she were content to sit by the fire, knitting or darning his socks, he could puff contentedly on his pipe and be quite happy. He turned his pockets inside out but was not rewarded with his pouch of tobacco.

"Doireann, have you seen my tobacco? I don't seem to have my pouch." Sean searched his pockets again and still found nothing.

"Do I look like I need to keep after your things on top of every-thing else I do around here? I cook, I clean, and now you want me to keep track of your belongings? Find it yourself or do without." She banged the dishes on the rough wooden shelf and turned her back on him.

Sean put his pipe back into his pocket and stepped outside to look for the errant pouch. *Must have dropped it on my way in*, he thought.

Doireann smiled grimly to herself and felt in her apron pocket for the pouch. *Serves him right,* she thought.

Sean had not always been so discontented. As a child, he ran and played with the other children, as lighthearted as any boy should be. He lived for festival time in the village, when tables laden with good food were set in the square, villagers brought out their instruments and played until dawn while the grownups danced, and the children played tricks on each other. While his mother was not well-off, neither did she lack for comfort and enough food to keep them both well-fed and happy. His mother, having lost her husband when Sean was just a babe, doted on him, a thin boy with mouse-brown hair and gray eyes. "You'll grow up to be something fine, you wait and see." She'd had faith in Sean, as every mother should have in her son.

All that changed when a young couple arrived in the village one cold winter's day. Walking behind a small cart from which dangled pots and pans, rattling and clanging with every step of the scrawny mule that pulled it, was a tall man dressed in black, brandishing a stick and with every other step striking the mule, as if he could encourage him to go any faster. The woman walked some steps behind, muttering to herself and peering out from under the shawl she kept wrapped around her head.

Sean's mother had stepped out onto their front porch and watched as they approached. *Who in heaven's name would be out on such a day as this?* she wondered to herself.

"Hello! Is anyone at home?" the man called out, as the cold wind sucked his words away.

"Hello yourself. Are you passing through?" Sean's mother asked.

"Indeed, but my poor mule is tired, and I fear we can go no farther. Would you let us camp here under your trees and rest?" he replied. The woman stood back from the cart and the man; she took no part in the conversation, instead eyeing the house and the rest of the village.

And so it happened that the couple camped by the house that Sean had been born in. They stayed for many more days than his mother had thought they would, but as time went on, the woman befriended Sean's mother, and gradually things began to change.

The man and his wife, not happy with camping under the trees, grumbled and complained so loudly that Sean's mother relented and invited them into her small cottage. Almost immediately, a change came over the home. While the woman seemed friendly, her sharp tongue and quick hand to reach out and pinch or slap were all that Sean felt. His mother began to neglect him; no more stories in the evening, no praise for chores done quickly, and no encouraging words to remind him that he was capable of great things. In fact, his mother began to criticize him and find fault with everything he did and said. Soon, it was clear that his mother had fallen under the influence of the woman, and her son's well-being no longer mattered to her.

As years went by, his mother kept more and more to herself, often sitting by herself, crying softly, or staring blankly into the fire, sipping at the strange dark tea the woman kept in front of her at all times. Sean would pull at her sleeves and beg her to come out into the garden, join the villagers in the square, do anything at all, but the only response he received was a blank look as she pushed him away. The villagers were puzzled by what they saw, but life was busy, and there was little time to consider the changes that had come over Sean and his mother.

The woman would sit by the fire, humming and combing her long black hair, hair so shiny you could see the light reflected in its tresses. His mother, once so happy to keep her house clean and neat, herself well-groomed and tidy, was set aside to make room for the woman with the long black hair. Over time, Sean learned to creep quietly into the house and keep to himself as much as possible. As he grew into a young man, his confidence faltered, and he stopped believing that he was capable of anything, much less something great or grand.

"You stupid dolt!" he heard most days. "Can you do nothing right?" A slap or a pinch was his reward if he asked for more food at the dinner table. He took to skulking in the corners or running outside as soon as he was dismissed from his chores. A child does not thrive without encouragement, and so it was that Sean did not grow to be a happy young man. He took to standing in the back of the crowd of villagers, stopped running and playing with friends, and spent most of his time alone and forgotten.

When it came time to find a wife, he was happy that Doireann would even look his way. She made it quite clear that he was not her first choice, and he would spend most of his days trying in vain to make her happy. When his poor, old mother passed away, he'd expected to bring Doireann to his family home, but the other woman had made it clear that she and the man would not be leaving now that they had a child of their own. He could go find his way in the world without their help, as far as she was concerned. He took to doing odd jobs around the village, built the small cottage that he and Doireann lived in, and spent his time longing for the time he'd felt loved and valued.

He turned his empty pipe over and over in his hands. *Maybe it would work*, he thought. *Maybe I could find a way to help and be somebody again.*

7
_____

TILLY

The next day dawned with a cold, bitter wind blowing down the valley from the mountains. It stripped the remaining fall leaves from the trees and sent them tumbling across fields and lanes in a confusion of browns and golds. Conor lay in bed listening to the wind scraping branches against his cottage roof, wondering why he could hear Wolf barking. "He's with Tilly," he muttered to himself. Rolling over and pulling his meager blanket tightly around him, he squeezed his eyes shut, determined to eke out any last remaining warmth before morning chores fired him out of bed.

A loud banging on his door ended any dream of more sleep. Insistent, almost violent, it sounded as if someone was determined to break down his door.

"Rust and buckets," he snarled. "May the devil take whoever it is that bangs on my door at this hour!"

Conor scrambled out of bed, thrust his feet into worn boots, and hobbled, still pulling them on, to the door. Throwing it open, the first thing he noticed was Wolf, who darted past him. "What in the name of the fates are you doing here, Wolf?" A whine answered him before Conor noticed the small crowd outside his door. Rubbing sleep from

34

his eyes, he found Tilly's father with his hand raised, ready to strike the door once more.

"Where is she?" the man demanded. Tilly's father, Quinn Mathuin, was a great, gruff man normally of good cheer, with always a kind word for Conor, a pat on the head for Wolf, and a poor joke or two that no one found very amusing. Known for his wisdom in solving the problems of their village, Quinn made a good partner to Erik Tamen, often providing the calm that Erik needed in the face of difficulties. Quinn loved nothing more than a quiet, peaceful home with a fire to sit before, tobacco to smoke in his pipe, and his Tilly to keep him company. He shared Tilly's blond hair, with his sweeping just at his shoulders and usually combed and brushed as much as any girl's. Today, his hair stood up in stalks, and there was no bit of cheer on his face as he once again demanded, "Where is Tilly? Is she here? What in all of creation is she doing here at this time of the day?"

Conor backed away from the doorway, the anger coming from Quinn like heat against his face. Confusion caused him to falter, questions flooded his mind, and he knew that something was terribly wrong, but he couldn't make sense out of anything.

"Tilly? Tilly isn't here! Why would she be here? We said good night last evening, and I sent Wolf to watch over her."

A thin woman with hair pulled back so tight her face seemed stretched pushed past the people on the steps and shoved Quinn out of the doorway. Molly Mathuin, Tilly's mother, was everything Quinn was not; bitter and angry, she blamed the world for her troubles. Her voice was never soft, always pitched in a constant whine that often rose to just short of a scream. "I would never let that fleabag of a mutt into my house, and you know it, Conor Matson! I threw him out the instant I saw him skulking around my front room. Why, in all that is holy, would you think I would allow that creature into my home? I knew Tilly was trying to sneak him in, but that won't happen as long as I am under that roof!" Her hands were clenched at her sides, and her face contorted into a snarl as she spat the words at Conor.

Conor held out his hands as if to ward off her angry words. He backed away from the door and reached to close it, when Molly shoved against it with her thin shoulder, catching him off guard and sending him to the floor. Wolf immediately rushed forward with a low growl, adding his voice to the confusion.

"Wolf! No! Down and back, boy!" Conor grabbed him from his place on the floor and pulled him to his chest. Wolf allowed himself to be pulled but never stopped the rumble that started deep in his chest and gathered strength as it rose through his throat.

Conor scrambled to his feet just in time to see Erik Tamen pushing his way through the crowd to join Quinn and Molly on his porch. "What's going on here, Quinn?" he asked. "I heard the yelling from across the village." Erik Tamen looked as disheveled as Quinn, his red hair sticking out every which way, his shirt only half tucked into his trousers, and his eyes bloodshot and weary from a night of little sleep.

"Tilly is gone, that's what's going on, Erik!" Quinn rubbed his hand across his face, as if he could wipe away the words coming from his mouth. "I went to her room to call her for an early breakfast. We were going to take our tea and biscuits outside to watch the sun come up. We planned it last night, but when I went to her room and knocked, she didn't answer, so I opened the door. Her bed was unmade, but she was not in it." His once angry voice now sounded lost and pathetic, and his eyes looked haunted. "I thought, just thought, that maybe she would have come here. Come to ask Conor to join us. My fear made me angry, Conor. But please tell me she came here this morning to ask you to join us. Please tell me that you sent her home and she's found a dozen things to distract her along the way. Please tell me that she left here and will be along home any moment now. Just tell me that, Conor, and I will leave you in peace." His voice sounded ragged, and his eyes pleaded with Conor to help him.

Conor hung his head, wishing more than anything that he could say those words to Quinn to reassure him that Tilly was fine and well on her way home. "I cannot say that, Quinn, for I've not seen Tilly since last evening. I swear to you that I sent Wolf to watch over her during the night, afraid that something might happen."

"What made you think that something might happen, Conor?" Erik Tamen looked puzzled.

"Something Granny Matilda said to us last night. More of a feeling than anything, sir. Not so much anything for certain, just a feeling." His look at Molly was full of recrimination. If she had let Wolf sleep beside Tilly's bed during the night, he was sure this conversation would not be taking place. This very sad man and angry woman would not be standing on his doorstep, and his Tilly, his friend, would be home, snug and safe.

The crowd outside Conor's cottage grew, and the low hum of the villagers' voices expressed their dismay. *Another child gone missing in the night. Tilly Mathuin this time? Not Tilly,"* they murmured to themselves.

At the edge of the crowd, a thin man with mouse-brown hair and watery eyes stood next to his stout wife. Doireann gripped Sean's arm tightly with her fingers. "See," she hissed. "This time it's Tilly gone in the night. The people won't stand for this. Say something, you! Speak up!" She continued to dig her fingers into his thin arm, as if she could infuse him with her determination.

Sean stepped forward. "What's this? Is Tilly missing? Has she disappeared along with the other children?" He raised his voice to be heard over the murmuring crowd. "Isn't it high time we did something? How many children are going to disappear before we act? Erik Tamen, you're the constable and the mayor. What do you plan on doing? We demand some answers. Why, we demand not just answers, but action, man! We put our trust in you, and look what it's got us? Nothing! Nothing but empty beds and broken hearts. I say it's time we came up with answers of our own!"

The murmurs of the crowd grew with every word Sean uttered, and people began looking at Erik with disapproval written clearly on their faces. *What has he done about this? Why, nothing, and it might be our children who disappear next! What about the families who've lost chil-*

dren? How is he helping them? The voices grew louder and the looks darker with each question.

Erik Tamen turned from Conor's porch to face the crowd. "Go back home now. Let us handle this." His words sounded weak even to himself.

"Handle this? Handle this how, Erik? You haven't handled anything so far, so now you want us to believe that you are going to start. I say someone else needs to be in charge of this, not you!" Sean flung the words toward Erik from his place in the crowd.

Erik fixed a look on Sean from the height of the porch. "If you think you can do better, Sean McCullogh, then get to it! I will hide and watch!" he roared.

Conor put his hand on Erik's arm and pulled him inside the cottage, gesturing for Quinn and Molly to follow. Kicking the door shut behind him, he turned to face them. "It's Tilly, Erik. Not some nameless child from across the village. This time it's Tilly who is missing. I don't mean to say they aren't important, but they aren't, not to me! They mean nothing to me! This means everything, Erik, everything!" Conor's voice broke over the words, and the look on his face was enough to make Erik take a step backward.

This from the boy who had been running wild through the village for more years than they could remember. The boy who raised himself and laughed at the villagers when they tried to take him in or do for him. The boy who seemed to let everything roll off him without its ever sinking in to make its mark. Now this boy stood with clenched fists and tears rolling down his face, every inch of his body held stiff and still.

Erik took in a ragged breath and let it out slowly. "You're right, son. I let my anger get the best of my tongue. I will look for Tilly, I promise. I talked with Granny Matilda just yesterday. She knows something, and I won't stop until she tells me what she's learned. I'll let you know what I find out, I promise. And I won't stop looking until I find her, son." He turned on his heel and went out the door, letting in a blast of cold air as he did.

Quinn sat down in Conor's chair by the fire, rubbing his hands over his face, as if he could wipe away the memory of the last hours. His face, once cheerful and friendly, now looked haggard and drawn. His eyes pleaded with Conor to tell him this was all a bad dream. Molly, standing with pursed lips, held her arms crossed tightly under her breasts. "I knew something like this would happen. I just knew it."

Quinn looked at his wife with surprise. "If you knew it, why in the devil didn't you let the boy's dog sleep by her side? What harm would it have done, woman? Maybe our Tilly would be laughing with us this very minute if you had given just a wee inch of space in your tight heart." Quinn rose from the chair with a groan and, without even looking at his wife, headed out the door. Passing Conor, he laid a rough hand on his shoulder and squeezed it tightly, so that Conor blinked in surprise.

Wolf gave a low growl as Molly took a step toward Conor. Conor stared at Molly without dropping his gaze, his anger burning brightly in eyes that brimmed with tears unshed. "You best go, Molly. Wolf doesn't take well to you." He turned his back on her and stared into the fire, determined that she not see the emotions running across his face. The slam of the door told him she was gone, and he let out the breath that he had been holding and collapsed into his chair. His hand reached down to settle on Wolf's head, the only source of comfort to Conor at this moment.

Erik Tamen made his way through the village toward the fields, beyond which lay Granny Matilda's tiny cottage. Walking through her front gate, he bellowed, "Granny! Granny! You and I need to talk! You're not going to want to hear what I say, but by the devil, you'll listen and give me some answers."

Before he reached her front steps, the door swung open, and there stood Granny, looking stricken, pale and tight-lipped. "It's true, isn't it? What I've seen? It's Tilly, isn't it?" Erik's affirmative nod was all it took for Granny to sway on her feet. He leaped forward to catch her as she fell to the porch floor.

Light as a feather she is, he thought as he carried her into the front room and laid her on the bed. She appeared not to be breathing, and he shook her slightly, as if to begin the process of drawing breath once more.

She gasped, and her eyes flew open. "Buckets of sheep dip," she groaned. "The devil take me for a weak old woman. Let me up, Erik, let me be." She pushed him back with an astonishingly strong arm and sat up, swinging her legs over the side. Her feet barely touched the floor, so small was she. "Tell me everything. Exactly as you know it."

"I got the word from the villagers, who heard the ruckus at the Mathuin household. Quinn and Molly were headed toward Conor's house, and I caught up as soon as I could. Quinn demanded to know where Tilly was, and Conor tried to explain that he hadn't seen her since last night, when he sent her home with Wolf to look after her. That blasted Molly sent the dog away, and now Tilly's gone as well!" He pulled his large hand through his red hair as if to pull it out in frustration and anger.

"I saw it coming, but I wasn't sure which one of the two it would be, Conor or Tilly. I figured wrong! I gambled, and I lost," she muttered.

"Explain yourself, woman!"

"Erik, I told you to watch the mountain, see the clouds swirling, dark and forbidding. There is a cave up there, and I believe the children sleep within that cave. They've been taken by a force that I don't understand, but I do know that someone controls that force, and they want our children for their own. I'm not sure why, and I'm not sure how. My sight doesn't always help me see everything clearly, but this I know. The children are there, and they sleep. So far, they have come to no harm, but I can't say that that will continue forever. They don't want them for any good purpose, this I know." Her voice was firm, her words clear and cold.

"Then that's where I go. To the top of the mountain, to the blasted cave, and get our babes back."

"Erik, you're going to need my help. Let me go with you. You know that I see things that you will never see or understand. I can help. I may be old, but I can still help."

He smiled at her sadly, thinking of the mountainous trails to climb, the cliffs, the rivers to cross, and the unknown waiting to be faced. "Granny, you and I have been crossways for a long time, and yet I know you to have a good heart. I'm just not sure your legs are as strong as your heart. I think this one I will have to do alone. I wish I could take your gift of sight with me, but never would it work."

He rose from the chair and, kissing her on the top of her head, left her cottage, closing the door so softly behind him.

"Stubborn old goat," she muttered. "Well, we'll see about that. My legs can still get me up the mountain, I believe!" She rose from her resting place and began assembling items, laying them out on the kitchen table: tea, wooden bowl and spoon, a small kettle, dried meat, bread and cheese. "Now where did I store those good, dried apples?" She found them in the back of the cupboard and added them to her pile. Stout shoes and woolen socks, a wool dress and cape, and finally a walking stick of the hardest oak, polished to a warm glow, were all added to the pile.

Just as she finished assembling her traveling goods, she heard footsteps on her porch. Yanking the door open, she held out her arms to the boy she knew would be there. Conor fell into her arms, sobbing and barely able to catch his breath. She held him tightly and patted his back, making soft soothing noises as she did. The minute he caught his first good breath, she pushed him away and held him at arm's length. "Now, you can continue to do that, or you can get ready to help me. Erik Tamen is leaving to find the children, and I mean to go with him, though he won't hear of it. I told him I was not too old for the journey or the trials that await us, but on second thought, I could use a hand to help me up the mountain. Will you come with me?"

Conor wiped the tears from his face with the back of his hand. "Only if Wolf can come too," he said softly.

"Wouldn't have it any other way," she grumbled. "I suppose I need to pack for you as well. Do you have a wool cape? Wool socks? Extra food?" At the sad shake of his head, she reckoned not. "I'll pack for us both."

Granny went back to rummaging through her cupboards and shelves until she had amassed a goodly pile of food and extra clothing. "Let's tie the extra clothing up in the capes, add the socks, and we should be ready for what that mountain throws at us. The food will go in our packs, along with my herbs and medicines. Oh yes, ointments. We'll need to take those as well."

8

ERIK TAMEN

E rik Tamen reached his house to find Guin packing clothes and food for him. "How did you know?" he asked as he pulled his cape tightly around him and took the large bundle of food from her hands.

She reached up to pat his face lightly with her worn hand. "As soon as the neighbors told me that it was Tilly this time, I knew you would be going straightaway. Not that the other children weren't equally important, but it is, after all, Tilly this time. I have food for three days at least, and if you take your bow with you, you might be lucky enough to shoot something to add to your dinner. Your knife is in the pack, as well as flint for your fire. Can you think of anything that I have forgotten, my love?"

He shook his head, wrapped his arms around her, and pulled her close, kissing the top of her head. "I don't know what I will find up there, Guin. Granny hasn't told me, for some reason. I can't figure why, but she thought if she didn't tell me, I would let her come with me. I won't. She isn't up for this kind of business, and in truth, she would just slow me down. I need to get to the top of the mountain as quickly as I can. She says the children are all there, unharmed. Why they don't just come home, I can't tell you, but I mean to find them and bring them home. Thank you for putting together food for me. I don't want you to worry about me, but I know that asking you not to worry is like spitting in the wind."

He kissed the top of her head again, mussed her hair, red with threads of gray running through it, and gave her one last tight squeeze before turning her loose.

She chuckled softly and laid her hand once more on his cheek fondly. "Spitting in the wind, Erik? How many times have I told you, you just end up wearing it? You go because it's your duty and because you care, but you, my love, better come back home to me, all in one piece! And bring our babies with you, please."

He gathered up his pack and closed the door quietly behind him. Stepping down off the porch, he turned and took a long look at the home he had shared with Guin for more years than he cared to think of. Rubbing his hand across his face, he headed down the worn dirt road leading out of the village toward the mountain, with its topmost peaks hidden in the dark clouds that never stopped roiling and swirling in an angry mass.

Erik Tamen had gone only a few steps when he heard his name called. Turning, he saw Sean and Doireann hurrying to catch him, she with skirts hitched high enough to show her stout legs pumping to keep up with her husband, and he red-faced and breathing hard. Erik Tamen put his pack down and waited for them to catch up, knowing that no good was going to come out of this encounter.

"I see you have decided to leave us," Sean snarled. "Are you ducking out before the rest of us drive you away?"

"What in blazes are you talking about, Sean? I'm going after the children. Granny Matilda thinks the children are at the top of the mountain, and I'm going there now." His tone was even but impatient. He never enjoyed talking with Sean, and Doireann made him weary to the bone with her constant nagging.

"Really? After all this time, now she tells you where our children are? If she knew, why didn't she tell us before now? Why wait? Why make us suffer and worry, if she's known all along? Why would she do that, Erik?" Doireann's voice rose higher with each question, until she sounded shrill and her eyes bulged slightly.

Erik sighed. "You know Granny has the gift of sight and healing. We've all experienced it at some time in our lives. But she can't always see things when she wants to see them. She can't always control it or make it happen when she wants it to happen. I don't know why she can tell me now where the children are and not yesterday or last month, but that's the truth of it. She's told me now, and I'm going to bring them home." He turned his back on them and gathered his things up from the road.

"Now, just you wait a minute, Erik!" Sean gripped his arm tightly. "Who's to mind the village business while you go hiding off to the devil knows where? Who's to see that the laws are kept and the dealings are fair?"

Erik Tamen shook off his hand and turned with a growl. "You do it. You've been wanting my job since the day they gave it to me. You do it, Sean, and hang yourself trying!"

"Well, I just thought that someone should have authority while you're gone. If you think I am the best man for the job, I'm happy to help, Erik," Sean purred and straightened his shirt, dusting off what he could to make himself look as presentable as possible. "I'll tell the council that you have asked me to take over while you're gone. Doireann can vouch for it. Right, sweet wife? I'll make good decisions, you'll see, Erik. You won't be disappointed that you chose me to be your successor." With that, he grabbed Doireann's hand and headed down the road toward the center of the village.

Erik Tamen shook his head in disgust. "I never meant for that to happen," he muttered, "but what harm can he possibly do in the couple of days that it will take me to climb the mountain and head back down with the children?" Erik Tamen adjusted his pack, shrugging his shoulders until it rode comfortably in place, and then, lengthening his stride, headed down the village road toward the fields beyond. *A day or two, three at the most,* he thought to himself as he stretched his legs and set his sights on the mountain in front of him.

Sean and Doireann fairly ran to the village center, faces turning red from the exertion and the excitement of the past few moments. "I knew it! I knew someday I would be the mayor and the constable. You wait and see, Doireann, I'm going to make some changes that the villagers will like so much that they'll want me to stay on and keep the job. They're tired of Erik and his jokes and his pats on the back and big laughs. They want someone who can get the job done, keep the village safe, and guard the children. I plan on making some big changes, you just wait and see!"

Doireann tried to answer, but for the first time in a while, she had no words to add. It could have been the sheer excitement of being married to the mayor, but most likely it was the pace that Sean set as he pulled her toward the village center that stole her breath and left her speechless. "Stop!" she finally managed to gasp out. "For the love of all that is holy, stop for a minute, Sean!" She dug in her heels and sat back, just about pulling him down in the effort.

He turned with a scowl before he remembered who he was dealing with at that moment. "Dear wife, forgive me. I'm eager to tell the villagers the news. I have so many great ideas in my head, and they are all bursting to get out. I want everyone gathered as soon as possible so that I can get started."

"That may be all good and well, Sean, but huffing and puffing and showing up red-faced with no breath left in our bodies is no way to call a meeting to order. Slow down and try to arrive with some level of dignity." She straightened her dress and tried in vain to put some order to her hair, smoothing it with both hands. Her chins quivered with each intake of breath, and her eyes bulged just a little as she tried to regain her composure.

"You're right, sweetheart. Of course, you're right. We should walk and arrive calmly and with confidence." He shoved his hands deeply into his pockets, straightened his shoulders, and lifted his head. Not in so many years had Sean felt this good, this happy. He would show them all that he was the more capable man. Erik was nothing but a bag of wind, a man happiest when he could stand outside someone's fence and visit and laugh with them. He, Sean, would have no time for that kind of idleness. He would set everyone to work immediately, cleaning up the village, cutting back the trees so that no creature could approach the village without their knowledge. Why, yes, he would set guards at night, and even during the day. He would drill the men and boys until they could learn to grab a pitchfork or a hoe and rush to protect the village against any intruder. He would insist that all the children sleep together in the church, with guards outside the doors. No one would get past them; no more children need disappear once he could lay down the law. The villagers just needed a firmer hand to guide them and laws that made sense. There would be no more gatherings, no more social times. It was time to prepare for the future and keep them all safe. He smiled to himself as he and Doireann walked sedately toward the center of the village.

9

A DECISION THAT COSTS

Granny finished filling her packs, one for her slight back to carry and a fuller one for Conor's. At the last minute, she made more packets of herbs to take along with them: healing herbs, herbs for sleep, and one that in a pinch would help her to see farther than she could on her own.

Conor, meanwhile, fidgeted and complained, "Granny, for all that is holy, don't you think you have enough for us to carry? How long do you plan on us being gone, after all? And where do you think my Tilly, our Tilly, is? You've never said, though you've dropped hints that you know. I want to know whatever it is you've learned with your gift of sight."

Granny sighed and sat down in her rocking chair by the fire. She looked at her hands, worn and wrinkled, and wondered if indeed she was up to the task. How could she tell Conor what she knew without breaking his heart, or worse, causing him to doubt her? How could she tell him about Mara and Jebez and all that she suspected she would find in that cave at the top of the mountain? She shook her head and gripped the arms of the chair with both hands. *I will tell him enough to give him heart but not enough to break his heart,* she told herself. "Conor, dear boy. The other day, before you and Tilly came to see me, I spent some time wandering in my mind. Do you know what that means?"

Conor shook his head. "Not really. I mean, I know that you can see things that aren't before you and things that haven't happened yet, but I don't know how you do it. I've just always believed in you, Granny. Partly because Tilly did, at least in the beginning. But now that I know you, I believe in you because of who you are. You've never lied to me or to Tilly. You've trusted us, and always given good advice when we need it."

"I don't plan on doing anything different now, but there are some things that I think but don't know. If I don't know it, I won't say it. Only if I'm sure. Does that make sense to you?"

Again, Conor shook his head. "Not really. I believe that you know things without really knowing them, without being sure. Granny, please don't keep me in the dark. It's Tilly! I'm not sure how to live without her, so anything you know or suspect, please tell me. I'm begging you!"

Granny took a deep breath and looked Conor squarely in his face. "I wandered in my mind, Conor, to the top of the mountain, and I think I found our children, all of them. Come outside with me, and let's sit on the porch for a bit, and I will try to explain."

Conor chafed at the delay but knew Granny well enough to know that he would never be able to harry her into leaving before she was ready. He followed her reluctantly to the porch and sat beside her in a worn wooden chair.

"Look up at the mountains, Conor. Tell me what you see there."

"The same old mountain that has been there since I can remember. It never changes; it's just a mountain," he said.

"Look again!" she demanded.

He did as she bade and stared hard at the mountain. He realized that she was right. There were thick black clouds, clouds that looked like they could rain down lightning and thunder, but the odd thing, he realized, was their constant movement. He squinted to see better. "The clouds," he said, "it looks like they are moving, but not in or out. Just around and around. I've never seen that before. Usually, they blow over the mountain and come down to our valley to bring weather, but those just look like they are blowing around and around the top of the mountain. That doesn't make any sense, Granny." He turned with a puzzled look on his face. "What does it mean?"

"I don't know the meaning of the clouds, but I suspect that they hold an evil in place. There is a cave at the top of the mountain, and I went there in my mind. The children are there, Conor. They appear to sleep, but I'm not sure what force holds them. I believe that Tilly is there as well. I think she sleeps along with the rest of our children. Something evil holds them, but I'm not sure what it is or who controls it."

"That doesn't make sense, Granny. Are you telling me that someone came down from that mountain, stole children—stole Tilly —out from under our noses, and took them all the way up that mountain? Who could do such a thing? Who could carry children up that mountain? Granny, you have to make sense, and you're just not doing that right now."

She sighed and reached over to hold his hand. "I'm not talking about a person, Conor. Not a person like you and I know. It's more like an evil presence, a thing without form or shape, that has our children, I believe. I told Erik Tamen that the children were there, and that's where he's going now. And if we are to go with him, we need to hurry along. I don't want him to leave without us. We are stronger when we are together, and we are going to need all the strength we possess if we are to win this battle."

She gathered up their belongings, giving Conor the lion's share to carry, took hold of her walking stick, and set out toward town and Erik Tamen's home at the center of it. Knocking on his door, she stepped back on the porch and waited for Erik or Guin to answer. She was not surprised when it was Guin who opened the door to her and Conor.

"He's gone, Granny. He left moments after he arrived back home. I think he knew that you were going to try to go with him, and he thought if he hurried, you'd be too late and wouldn't follow."

"Sheep's dip to that, Guin! I know the way better than he does, and I know better than he what waits for him at the mountaintop. Hang him for leaving without us!" she growled and stepped back off the porch.

"Us?" Guin looked puzzled.

Conor stepped forward. "I'm going too. He had to know that I would want to come as well. I could not do anything but come!" His voice rang loud and clear.

Guin sighed. "No, of course you couldn't, Conor. You've loved Tilly since you knew what love was, and maybe even before. But, Granny, let's be honest here. You're old, and he's far too young to take this on. I'm worried about my husband as it is, and if I knew you were following him, I wouldn't rest a bit. Why don't you stay here in the village and wait for Erik to come back? I think that would . . ."

The look that Granny shot Guin stopped the words in her mouth. "Sheep's dip!" she said and turned on her heels. "How long ago did he leave? Will you at least tell us that?"

Guin shook her head. "Within the hour."

"Good, we have a fair chance of catching up to him if we leave this minute."

Once again, Granny gripped her walking stick tightly and set out at a brisk pace, so brisk that Conor had to take a few skipping steps to catch up to her. They hadn't reached the edge of the village when a frantic voice reached their ears. "Granny, Granny Matilda! Please stop. Please wait!"

Granny turned to see a young girl, skirt hitched to her knees, braids flying out behind her as she ran down the dirt path. When she caught up to them, she leaned forward, hands on her knees, gasping for breath. Granny waited impatiently for her breath to catch enough for her to speak. "What is it, child? We're about to leave, and we're in a bit of a hurry."

"It's my ma, Granny. The baby's coming early. She said I was to fetch you no matter what. She's in a lot of pain, and she says something's not right. The baby is too early, and things don't feel right inside of her, she says. She says you need to come quickly. Please, Granny!"

"Well, the devil take this if he pleases. What am I to do?" She leaned on her walking stick and set her eyes on the distant mountain. Chewing on her lower lip, she looked at the young girl and then at Conor. "You know what I have to do, don't you, Conor? I'm the only source of herbs and healing this village has. I made a vow years ago that I would do whatever I could to help my friends and neighbors. Now I am tested more than I ever thought possible. My Tilly against the life of a young mother and perhaps her baby. How do you balance that, Conor? How do you choose?"

"Granny, there's no choice. You have to go after Tilly. Someone else can help this girl's mother. There are lots of women in the village who know how to have babies. They do it all the time. I think there is only one choice, and that's the one we were on. Now let's get going." He looked at the girl just once and turned his back on her.

Granny reached out and grabbed his arm. "No, Conor. I meant the only thing I can do is stay here and help. I cannot leave without making sure I've done everything possible for this girl's mother. I'm sorry. I hope you understand, but my vow must not be broken."

He shook off her arm. "No, I don't understand. I don't even know this girl or her mother, and maybe you don't either. We need to leave now, or we won't be able to catch Erik Tamen. Granny, come on!" His eyes pleaded as much as his voice did.

"I'm sorry. We'll go after Erik later. I promise. But healing comes first," she spoke sadly, knowing that he was too young to understand her decision. "Show me the way," she commanded the girl.

Conor watched in disbelief as Granny and the girl headed back to the village. He looked at Wolf, who gave no indication that he understood any more than Conor did. "Hang it all, Wolf! I don't know the paths up the mountain. I have no idea what direction he went. I don't know how to follow without her. Hang her for a stubborn old woman. If anything happens to Tilly, forgiveness won't even be talked about!" He picked up the pack of supplies and followed after Granny and the girl.

10

THE WRONG PATH

Erik Tamen reached the end of the valley by midday. He found an old elm tree with drooping branches to settle under and opened his pack to see what his dear Guin had packed. He pulled out cheese wrapped in cloth, bread still warm from the oven on the inside, and some dried apples. He left the mutton for his dinner and tucked into the cheese and bread. "No one bakes bread like Guin does," he said to no one, for no one was anywhere near him. He leaned against the trunk of the tree and gazed up at the range of mountains in front of him.

For the most part, the mountains seemed quiet and without cause for alarm. It was the peak in the middle, where the range came together to form the highest part, that held his attention. The black clouds still swirled constantly around the top, never blowing away, just moving around and around, as if pulled by an invisible string or controlled by a breath too strong for human lungs. *What the devil could it be? What could hold those clouds there for days on end?*

He stopped his musing, carefully packed up the remainder of his food, and, grabbing up his walking stick, got slowly to his feet. *Time to go. Those children aren't going to come down from the mountain on their own.*

The path, worn mostly by the hooves of deer or mountain goats, took him gradually up out of the valley and into the low hills. They stretched out lazily in front of him, seemingly low and without the need for much effort to climb them, but that was a trick of the eye, comparing them to the mountains beyond, for soon Erik was stopping to catch his breath and had need of his stout walking stick much more than he planned on doing.

He continued to climb the hills, threading his way across small valleys tucked between them, fording streams, from which he filled his bottle as often as he could, and stopping now and then to look back on the trail behind him. He didn't really think that Granny would be on the trail, but he found himself half hoping that he would see her frail body and her face with that determined scowl on it. He discovered that he was disappointed not to see her, an emotion he'd never expected to feel. What was it about that old lady, that he found he needed her, even when it killed his soul to do so? Did he have confidence in her that he denied having?

He thought about the days following the death of his son, the death that Granny had foretold. He searched his memory for the exact words she'd used, her tone, and the message that she brought to him and Guin. Did she think that the telling would somehow keep the child safe from harm? Did she think it was a warning that they could heed and do something to prevent his death? He thought back to the first small cough the boy gave, the first hint of fever in the small body. He knew that he and Guin had done everything they could to save him, everything but the one thing that Guin wanted him to do— seek Granny's help. After her words, he wanted nothing to do with her, much less have her anywhere near his son. But now, so many years later, when it was far too late to remedy the situation, he couldn't help but mull it over in his mind as he climbed the hills, coming closer to the mountains with every step.

Was he just a stubborn fool even then, too stubborn to keep his only son alive? No, if he thought she could have helped with her basket of herbs and her poultices laid on chests, he would have done it. He would have sought her out, but those herbs just made terrible-tasting teas, and the poultices stank so badly, you couldn't be in the same room with them. No, once the coughing and the fever started, the child was lost within days, and there was no one, not Granny, not anyone, who could have reversed the course that the fates had set for him and Guin.

It was with these dark thoughts clouding his mind that he began to climb the trail up the mountains. Rocky and narrow, the trail wound around and up. Scattered pines and low bushes grew beside the trail, giving little shelter from the sun overhead. He stopped to take a cloth from his pocket and wipe away the sweat that stung his eyes and trickled down his face. This time of the year, the day could begin with a cold wind from the north and end with the hot sun warming the air. Turning, he looked back down into the valley, enjoying the sight of the village so far in the distance he had to squint to make out any of the shapes below.

Once again, he started up the trail, using his stick to help him navigate the steepest parts, the twists and turns. The pines grew smaller and more stunted the farther he climbed, the bushes fewer between the trees. He realized that he no longer heard birds singing or the hum of insects. *Why is it so quiet?* he wondered. Had it always been this quiet since he started climbing? He stopped once more in the shade of the tallest pine he could find and listened carefully. No, not one sound did he hear. That wasn't natural. Even with the sound of his feet on the path, there should have been noises all around him. There was no buzzing, no chirping, no creature scurrying to get out of his way. Nothing but the utmost quiet.

The path took him around and back again, in such a way that he never had to climb straight up but instead wound back and forth in a switchback pattern that made the trail so much longer but less steep. He stopped as evening began to settle and once again rummaged through his pack for food. *I'll eat just a bite and then climb a little farther and find a place to spend the night. Funny, I thought I would have reached the cave that Granny told me about by now. It must be farther than she thought, or I've gotten off track somehow. No sense getting lost up here. I'll stop for the night and set out first thing in the morning.*

He gathered his things, stuffing them into his pack, and set off once again. This time the trail took him to the edge of a sharp cliff, beyond which lay the mountain. *Hang it*, he thought. *I'm going to have to find a way around this or down it before I can go any farther.*

The cliff ended abruptly over a sharp cut in the side of the mountain, thick with undergrowth and rocks long tumbled down from the sides of the mountains. He tied his pack over his shoulder, and setting his walking stick on the ground, lay face down on the edge of the cliff with his legs dangling over the edge. Carefully, slowly, Erik inched his way to the edge. Swinging his feet down, he felt carefully for any kind of foothold, something to wedge his foot into to give himself some stability while his hands held onto the sparse growth of bushes near him. Searching blindly with the toe of his boot, he found a small ledge, small enough for a mouse to sit on, but big enough for just the toe of his boot. Testing it gingerly with half of his weight only, he felt a good, solid base underneath him. He lowered himself just a little and began feeling with the toe of his other foot. Nothing! His arms ached with the effort of holding himself on that one toe as he searched for anything to rest the other half of his weight on. Sweat gathered on his forehead and trickled into his eyes. He lowered himself just a hair, giving that foot new territory to explore. He was rewarded with another good ledge, this one even bigger than before. With two feet somewhat firmly planted, he lowered himself still more, the fingers of his right hand digging into the rock for any kind of hold, the left still gripping the bush above. Sweat once more stung his eyes, and he wanted more than anything to wipe it away, but his hands were full, and all he could do was blink it away.

Hand over hand, one foot at a time, he crept down the side of the cliff, like some huge insect walking backward. Every now and again, he would stop to catch his breath and lean his head as close to his shoulder as he dared to wipe the sweat away. Bit by bit, he continued his painful journey down the cliff, feeling with the toes of his boots, searching with his fingers for any hold he could find. His fingers ached with the effort, and cramps began to stiffen his hands and legs. He stopped more often now, wishing he could flex his fingers for just a moment, stretch his legs, and wiggle his feet. His right foot found yet another ledge, and he tried putting more of his weight on it to relieve the pain in his left leg. Just as he did, he felt the smallest, barest give to the rock he'd rested his foot on. Quickly, he dug his fingers in and threw his left leg back against the cliff, but it was too late.

The rock gave way, and despite his hands scrabbling to find a hold, he felt himself begin to slide down the side of the cliff toward the rocks below. Desperately, he grabbed at every rock he slid past but was rewarded only with dirt and rocks raining down on him. *Oh, Guin, I am so sorry,* was his last thought as he fell, hitting the tree branches below before coming to rest between two rocks. A groan escaped his lips, and then darkness and the relief from pain that it brought swept over him.

11

GRANNY TRAVELS

Conor sat with his back against the wall and his legs stretched out on the porch in front of him, one arm wrapped around Wolf's shoulders, the other tapping the floor impatiently. Every now and then, a deep sigh emerged from the boy, but other than that and the tapping, he was still and quiet, watching the mountain in the distance. His eyes stayed on the swirling dark clouds, and he wondered if Tilly really was there. Was she sleeping, as Granny thought? Was she hurt? Was she scared? No, he thought, she would not be scared. She would be fierce as always. He had never known anyone as brave as Tilly.

He remembered back to the time Tilly had gone with him to gather Granny's sheep, high up in the hills. They had wandered farther than ever before in search of good grazing, and it took them a while and miles of walking before they found them in a deep, narrow valley. The rainwater had filled the space, and after it receded, deep, green grass grew there. The sheep were delighted with their find and grabbed mouthfuls of the sweet, sun-drenched grass. So busy and happy were they that they failed to notice the small pack of wolves watching them from the top of the hills.

Conor and Tilly arrived in time to watch the wolves begin their descent toward the sheep at the bottom. Tilly gasped when she saw the scene before them and, without hesitation, started running down the side of the hill toward the sheep. "Wait, Tilly! Wait!" Conor had hollered at her. She slid to a stop and turned toward him, questions written across her face and a scowl etched in her forehead.

"If you scare them, Tilly, the sheep might just run away from us and toward the wolves. We need to be quiet and somehow get between the sheep and the pack."

Tilly had nodded her agreement and fell in behind Conor as he crept to the side of the hill and began circling behind the sheep. She picked up rocks along the way, stuffing them into the pockets of her skirt, until it looked as if her skirt would drag to the ground with the weight. Slowly, carefully, they picked their way through the bushes and grass until they reached the far side of the flock.

"Now!" yelled Conor. He stood up and waved his arms at the sheep to run them back the way they had come. Tilly, meanwhile, stood her ground and began throwing her rocks as hard and fast as she could at the wolves. One caught a wolf square between his eyes, causing him to yelp in pain and stop any forward motion. He shook his head to relieve the pain, but Tilly caught him once again on the side of his head, and that was enough to convince him that retreat was the better order of the day. There would be no mutton for his dinner. The others quickly followed suit, with Tilly running behind them, pitching rocks as fast as she could pick them up off the ground!

When she turned to find Conor and the sheep, her face was split with the biggest grin he had ever seen. "Now that was fun!" she exclaimed.

There was no doubt in Conor's mind. If there were an opportunity and any rocks within her grasp, Tilly would be wreaking havoc no matter where she was. That girl had deadly aim. Conor rested his head on the wall behind him and closed his eyes. The faintest smile crossed his lips as he thought about his friend, and soon his head began to nod forward, and his body relaxed in sleep.

Inside the cottage was a scene less quiet and still. Granny Matilda hovered over a young woman on her side on a rough bed. She rubbed her back with liniment made from comfrey and lavender. A blackened pot filled to the brim with water sat on the hearth, steaming and bubbling gently. Fresh linens lay on the table next to the bed, ready whenever Granny knew the time was near. A small groan escaped the woman's lips, and then she pressed them quickly and tightly together to stifle any further noise.

"Breathe," Granny commanded. "Just breathe, shallow and fast like I taught you before. Remember when you had this sweet girl sitting over there? You used breath to help ease the pain. The comfrey will help with the pain, and the lavender will calm. Now, just breathe!"

The woman obeyed, breathing short, hard breaths, and Granny felt her relax under her touch. "Good!"

Granny had brought most of the village babes into the world, helping mothers young and old safely through the birth of their wee ones. Seldom had she lost a baby or mother in all those years, and she was determined that tonight would be no different. Her calmness, her skill with herbs, and her knowledge of the ways to help with pain added to her reputation among the villagers. No one hesitated to call on her, no matter the hour of day or night, because they knew in their hearts that despite the grumbling and muttering, Granny would have been furious to know that someone had tried to do it without her. She took pride on feast days, counting all the little ones running across the square, squealing with laughter, knowing that she had helped bring them to this life.

The night wore on, and she kept up the pressure on the woman's back, rubbing and kneading away the aches and pains. She gave her herb tea to sip on to ease the pain and help to calm her. In Granny's mind, a calm mother was a good mother. And a calm birth was a much better birth than any other. Granny stopped occasionally to rub her own back and straighten up. "Erik's right," she muttered. "Not as young as I used to be!"

The sun had begun to lighten the sky in the east when at last a small baby boy, wrapped in clean white linen, was placed in his mother's arms. Granny took a piece of wet linen and wiped the woman's brow and gave her more tea to drink. "Drink all of this, every bit," she demanded of the woman. "It will make everything so much easier as the days go on. I will leave a packet on the table. Make sure you brew more twice a day and drink every bit of it."

She began gathering her belongings, making sure that her medicines and herbs were carefully packed away in her pack. She stopped long enough to rouse the young girl who had brought her to the cottage. "You have a baby brother, Sister. Look after your ma, make sure she drinks two cups of the tea that I left, and be a good sister to your baby brother."

Granny stepped out on the porch into the soft morning light. She gazed down at Conor, who had slumped over and now lay across Wolf, snoring softly. She wondered if he would ever understand her decision to stay the night and help the woman and her child. Would it make a world of difference to Tilly? Would they be able to find Erik Tamen and join him on his mission to bring the children home? Would this ache in her back subside enough to allow her to climb to the top of the mountain? She longed for a cup of the tea that she had brewed inside the cottage to ease the stiffness and shooting pains she felt in her lower back. She rubbed her back once more and thought of going back to her cottage for more liniment and tea.

Taking her eyes off Conor and Wolf, she looked at the distant mountain. *I need to be able to travel there before we go. I think I will tell Conor that I need to go back to the cottage before we set off. I might be able to find Erik, and that would give us a better chance of catching up to him.*"

She bent down and softly shook his shoulder. His brown hair had fallen across his forehead, and she brushed it back and away from his eyes. *How small he is,* she thought to herself. *How on this good green earth can I ask him to help me get Tilly back?*

She shook Conor once more, and he opened his eyes slowly, trying to figure out where he was and why Granny was shaking him. As soon as his eyes opened fully, he jumped to his feet. "Are you ready?" he demanded. "Are you ready now to do what's right and go find Tilly?" He grabbed up the pack and walking stick that lay at his feet. His eyes on Granny were hot with anger, and his voice was rough.

She sighed. "Yes, Conor, but first, I must go back to my cottage. I'll explain everything when we get there. I know you'll try hard to understand."

Once again, she walked off without looking back at him. He opened his mouth to rebuke her but realized she was rapidly going beyond the hearing of his voice. "Hang her, Wolf! She can't keep walking off without us. Let's go see what she wants to do now."

Conor and Wolf reluctantly followed down the path that led to Granny's cottage at the edge of the village.

Once at the cottage, Granny refilled her pack with comfrey and lavender for liniments and tea for aches and pains. She thought briefly of brewing herself a cup but figured that that would be beyond Conor's capacity for patience.

"Conor, there's something that I would like to do, if you will allow me to do it." Her request was made in a soft voice that caught Conor off guard. It was the same voice she had used the night that Tilly was taken. The voice she'd used to warn them and ask them to look after each other. And it was a voice that no matter how angry he was with her, he could not ignore. It was so close to pleading, something that Granny Matilda never, ever did.

"Yes, Granny. You know that I'm not going to stand in the way of what you need to do. I might be angry with you for helping that woman and delaying us, but I'm not stupid enough to think that you don't know what you're doing when it comes to looking for Tilly." He sat down in the chair by the fire and waited for her to tell him what she needed to do.

"I know that you are aware that I can sometimes see things and that I know things that other people don't know. Things that haven't happened yet or things that happen a good distance away from here. Let me explain the best that I can how it works. I travel, Conor, but only in my mind. My body stays right where it is, thank the fates, or I doubt I'd be able to do it at my age. I can't explain it fully, only that I sit still and concentrate. I empty my mind of all thoughts and concerns. Memories fade, as do daily worries and the things that pester our minds. I empty my mind and then fill it with a vision of quiet water; a pond, a lake, or a very still river, it doesn't matter.

"Once my mind is full of that vision, then it is free to wander. I can direct it by thinking of what I am looking for. For instance, when I traveled the last time, I thought of the missing children. I emptied my mind, filled it with the sight and sound of water, and then thought of the children. Before I knew it, I had traveled to the top of the mountain, where I found a cave. As soon as I realized where I was, I sensed the danger that lay within that cave. The air was cold against my skin, but that isn't what raised goose bumps along my arms and legs and made the hair on the back of my neck prickle. It was the presence of evil within the cave that did it. Oh, Conor, I was so frightened. Never have I encountered pure evil like I felt that day at the entrance to the cave. I wanted nothing more than to flee down the mountain and return to my safe cottage and forget everything I felt there. But I knew that I had to see for certain that the children were there, so I crept, like some pitiful little mouse, into the cave until I found them. Body after body, asleep, covered with cloth, breathing slowly and softly. Alive but in such a deep sleep that I'm not sure they could be roused. I found not only the children but someone looking after them, if that's what you could call what she was doing."

"She?" asked Conor. "Did you recognize her?"

"Yes, I think I did," she answered softly, looking into the far distance. "At any rate, I would like to travel now and see if I can find Erik Tamen. If we knew where he was, it would be so much simpler to join him rather than stumbling around on the mountain stupidly."

"Granny, you dodged my question quite neatly. But yes, of course you should try to find him. Will I bother you if I sit here with you? Should Wolf and I go outside?"

She reached out and patted his hand. "No, stay, please. It would be a comfort to have you here in case I am frightened." She sat back in her chair and closed her eyes.

She emptied her mind completely, setting aside thoughts of Tilly, the villagers, the children, and even Conor, who sat across from her.

She pictured a small stream, quietly bubbling across rocks and around clumps of grass growing at its edge. Her mind followed the stream as it picked up a leaf or insect and carried them softly away. Slowly, her mind emptied, until the only thing was the water, softly, slowly moving through space and time. When nothing occupied her mind but the water, she began to think of Erik Tamen. She thought of his red hair and beard, his loud voice, his abrupt but friendly manner. Slowly, her mind began to travel through the valley toward the mountains.

She saw where he'd sat under an elm tree and eaten his midday meal. She followed him up the switchback trail, climbing back and forth, higher and higher. She paused where he had eaten his evening meal and pondered where he might have gone next. Had he bedded down here for the night? Had he traveled just a bit farther before darkness descended?

She continued on the trail, coming at last to the edge of the cliff. Staring down over the side, she saw the split in the earth below that created a narrow valley, strewn with rocks and scrubby trees. *Where could he have gone from here?* she wondered.

Her eyes searched the valley below, the sides of the cliff, as much as she could see but came up with no hint of the man. Puzzled, she turned to walk back down the trail, when she caught a glimpse of a polished piece of wood at the edge of the cliff. Too smooth to be a branch, too worn to be anything but a walking stick. She bent to touch it and was immediately overcome with a vision of Erik Tamen sliding down the side of the cliff, heading toward the rocks below. Gasping, she ran back to the edge and looked down. No sign of him anywhere that her poor eyes could see. Her mind traveled down to the valley floor, a much easier task when her body could stay put where it was. Looking carefully, she noted broken branches on a tree or two. *He must have fallen,* she thought to herself. *Why would he try to climb down that cliff? Why not just go back down the trail and find a way around this cut?*

Granny felt herself being pulled back as these thoughts began to crowd her mind. She stopped and visualized the stream once more to quiet her mind and her thoughts. Once again, she found herself at the bottom of the cliff, this time looking at stains on the rocks. She stretched out a hand to touch the rock. Nothing came away on her hand. She looked around wildly, thinking she would see Erik hobbling along, wounded but able to walk. Nothing! No Erik, no sounds, no nothing. She emptied her mind once more, filled it with the quiet water, and then thought of Erik, perhaps hurt and unable to travel. Her mind traveled without her directing it, moving across the mountains, searching for any sign of the man. Nothing!

She was about to give up, when she sensed more than saw hands lifting Erik, bringing a cup to his lips. "The Mountain Folk," she gasped. "He's with the Mountain Folk!" Her mind began the swift journey down the mountain, to where her frail body sat by the fireplace in her cottage. Back at the cottage, her eyes flew open, and she stared at Conor.

"Did you find him?" he demanded.

"Not exactly. I don't know exactly where he is, but I think I know who he is with right now." She got up from her chair and started for the small kitchen area. Opening her cupboards, she rummaged around until she found what she was looking for and stuffed it in her pack with the rest of her food and herbs.

"I don't understand. Did someone go with him? Is he with the children? Stop! Answer me, hang it!"

"I will. I promise. I will tell you everything I know and everything I suspect. But I think we should leave now. I think he might be in danger. I'll tell you everything as we walk, I promise!"

She grabbed up her pack and her walking stick and left through the door, letting Conor and Wolf close up the cottage and follow her.

12

THE SEARCH FOR ERIK TAMEN

"Granny, wait! For the love of all, wait for us!" Conor felt silly asking an ancient woman to wait for him and Wolf, but Granny's skinny little legs were moving so fast that he had to run to catch up to her.

"Conor, I don't have time to wait. Erik might be in danger, and if nothing else, I believe he is seriously injured." Her voice was strong, no sign of the huffing and puffing that Conor was doing to maintain the pace.

How does she do that? he thought to himself as he lengthened his stride to keep up with her. "You said you would explain this while we walked, so let's hear it. Where is Erik Tamen, and why do you think he might be injured?"

"I traveled up the mountain and found his trail pretty easily. He'd been on the switchback, a trail that I wish he hadn't used, because it dead ends at a cliff that is nearly impossible to climb down. This is why I wish he had waited for us. I might not know a lot, but hang it all, I know these mountains. I used to run all over them with my father as a young girl. My father hunted, and when he wasn't hunting here, he was always searching for new game trails. He allowed me to come with him because I was fast and quiet. Oh, how I loved exploring these mountains with him. And just like a memory, the trails came back to me as if I had climbed over them just yesterday, not fifty years or more ago.

"At any rate, I knew that switchback trail to be a dead end, and if I had been with Erik, I would have told him that, and we could have found a better trail to take, one that would have had us up the mountain a lot sooner. I tracked him there and knew by the walking stick I found at the edge of the cliff that the fool man had tried to climb down. A fool's errand if ever there was one. I followed him to the bottom of the cliff; it's a narrow valley with rocks that slid down the mountain eons ago. Some brush and small trees make the rocks and boulders hard to see, but I found what I was looking for. Rocks with what looked like fresh blood on them. Any blood that had been there for a while would have been washed away by the rains and covered with last year's snow and long faded. This blood was not faded. Bright red and fresh to my eyes." Granny stopped to catch her breath. Walking was fine but walking and talking took far more effort than she cared to admit.

"Blood? But what about Erik Tamen? Was he there? Did you look?" Conor questioned.

"Of course. Don't take me for an idiot, Conor. An old woman, perhaps, but not an idiot. I looked all around, and there was no sign of him, but I did see where someone might have dragged him off the rocks and through some of the bushes, and I had to ask myself, 'Who would be up the mountain, to find him and take him away?' Only one group of people that I know about know this mountain like I do: the Mountain Folk." Granny said this through clenched teeth, as if the very words were bitter.

"I've heard of the Mountain Folk, Granny, but surely I thought it was just stories to scare us. Tilly used to tell me about them around the fire at night, as if she could ever scare me with children's stories of boogiemen in the mountains."

"They're more than stories, Conor. The Mountain Folk are real, but we stopped talking about them, for the most part, years ago. I wonder where Tilly heard the stories she told. Or did she just hear about them and make up her own stories? Wouldn't put it past that girl to come up with her own stories. No one has an imagination like she does!"

Granny, Conor, and Wolf continued along the path that led through the valley and toward the low hills at the foot of the mountains. Granny slowed her pace to allow her breath to catch up so she could keep her promise to Conor and tell him as much as she could at the moment. The sun was warm on their backs, and Wolf left the trail often to chase rabbits or squirrels, always rejoining them before they were too far down the path. The pace was one that they both could keep up for hours, stopping now and again to drink water and look around them.

"So, you think Erik Tamen tried to climb down the cliff and fell? You think he was badly hurt?" So many questions crowded Conor's mind.

"I'm pretty sure that's what happened. I think he left his walking stick at the top because he couldn't carry it and his pack and climb down at the same time. It looked to me like there were loose rocks at the bottom near where I found the blood on the rocks. I can't say for certain that he brought them down when he fell, but it seems like a good guess to me. At any rate, let's stop here for our meal, and I will tell you about the Mountain Folk."

They settled under an elm tree much like the one that Erik Tamen took his midday meal under and took out bread and cheese and fruit from their packs. Conor dug in as if he hadn't eaten in days, and Granny watched him with a half smile and thought, *I forget that this boy lives on his own. It's a wonder he has any meat on his bones at all. When this is over, I need to remember to have him to supper a few times a week.* She nibbled at some cheese and broke off a small bit of bread.

"Can we afford to sit here long?" asked Conor. "You said he could be in danger!"

"We'll eat and quickly, then move on toward the hills. I don't think I can find the Mountain Folk before dark. We'll have to sleep where we can and then find them in the morning."

She leaned against the trunk of the tree and stretched her legs out to the sun. She wiggled her shoes back and forth, stretching her ankles as she closed her eyes.

"The story started years ago, long even before I was born." She spoke softly, with her eyes still closed, as if bringing memories up from the past. "They didn't always live in the mountains; in fact, they lived in the valley, where we live still to this day. Their village was a few leagues from ours. But while our village grew and prospered, their village suffered greatly. Their crops failed, their children took sick, cows would not produce milk, sheep died unexpectedly— nothing seemed to go well for them.

"At first our village tried to help them. Our villagers took seeds to replace the ones they lost when their crops failed, nursed their children through illness, and tended to their flocks.

"The men stood guard with them against wolves, they thatched their roofs when the storms blew through, and the women shared whatever extra food they had as often as they could. But it got to be too much. No matter how many times our village helped them, it was never remembered or appreciated. It got so they expected us to carry them through storms, failed crops, and wild animals that ravaged their flocks and herds of cows."

Granny sighed, and her voice sounded sad to Conor's ears. "After a time, our own village began to suffer as a result of all the help that was at first freely given. Over time, the children began to go hungry as the stores of food dwindled. The crops were not as full as they had been. The men had little time to tend their own fields for helping the others. The women neglected their children to tend to the babies and young ones of others. It couldn't last. It was no way to live, for either village. I don't know if it was just plain bad luck or if there was laziness and neglect to blame, but the folk began to resent the help given to them. It's a funny thing about too much help. At first, it seems like a good thing. But then, when you rely on it too much, you don't like it. You resent the help and the people giving it, but it's a habit that you can't break. Habits are funny things; first cobwebs and then chains, Conor. The habit of taking help began to be like chains that kept them from doing things on their own, I'm afraid.

"Our village ordered a council meeting, and the men and women talked about solutions for hours. No one wanted to walk away from these poor folk, but everyone had a story to tell of ingratitude on the part of the people, and stories of our own houses with leaking roofs and crops rotting in the fields for no one to gather them."

Granny packed the leftover food into their packs and, gathering her walking stick, set out toward the hills with Conor in step and Wolf trailing behind.

"That still doesn't explain how the Mountain Folk came to be up there." He nodded toward the mountains looming closer with every step they took.

Granny followed his gaze and shook her head. "That's not the whole story. The villagers left the meeting still undecided about the future and how to deal with the folk down the valley. They met the next day and the next, but still no one came up with a solution."

Granny continued, "In the meantime, no one was going to the village down the valley. They were too busy trying to come up with an answer they could all live with. A few days into it, there came a delegation of the other folk demanding to know where the villagers had been and why they hadn't been coming to tend the crops, mend the roofs, and heal the sick.

"Mouths agape, the villagers listened to their demands, shuffling their feet and looking at the ground, from what I heard. Finally, the mayor stepped forward and ordered them to stop—stop talking, stop demanding, stop expecting. He told them that they had been meeting for days, trying to figure out how to help them and still keep their own village going. The end of it was, they couldn't do both. He told them it was time they looked after themselves, took care of their own business, and left his people alone. There were harsh words spoken by both sides, I suppose. Threats were made and curses were leveled at our villagers, but they stood their ground and refused to budge. They all stood behind the mayor like a solid wall, staring down at the folk."

"I see why they would be angry and disappointed, but they had to know our villagers couldn't keep helping them forever. That still doesn't explain how they came to be called Mountain Folk." Conor shook his head as he said this.

She sighed "Sadly, that's not the end of the story. Things went from bad to worse, as they sometimes do. Before long, there were fires in the hay fields and sheep gone missing or found dead. Outlying cottages were broken into, and one even burned to the ground. No one could prove that it was the folk from down the valley, but who else would it have been? The mayor and a delegation of council members went to the folk to talk with them. They were met with men carrying pitchforks and shovels standing along the road, watching them with sullen faces, and finally a rock was thrown. It only takes one, Conor. One stupid fool to pick up one stupid rock and throw it, and the dam bursts.

"Before the mayor and the council members could turn around, all the folk were throwing rocks, many of them finding their marks. The mayor and the council got away, but not before many of them had cuts and bruises all over. One councilman fell as he tried to get away from the rocks and broke his arm. Now we had real damage done to our villagers."

The path through the hills wound around and up toward the mountains beyond. The grass was thick and green here, with low bushes, and tall trees shaded them from the sun. The hum of bees and insects kept them company, along with the occasional birdsong that trilled across the hills. Conor kept pace with Granny and listened eagerly to her story, wondering still how it tied into Erik Tamen, who had gone missing.

Granny was silent for a while, concentrating on her mission to reach the mountains before dark overtook them. "The rest of the story is hard to tell, Conor, because it doesn't reflect well on our village." She paused and gathered her thoughts, thinking of how to explain what happened next.

"Once again, our village met, but this time they were angry. It's hard not to be angry when you've tried to help someone and are rewarded with evil. I'm not saying what they did was right, no sir! I'm just trying to get you to understand why they did it." She sighed and looked pained.

Conor stopped on the trail and took her arm. "They did something to the other folk, didn't they, Granny? They were fed up and angry and maybe a little scared of what would happen if they didn't do something."

"Yes, Conor. The men of the village gathered in force and marched to the folk down the valley. They drove them out of their homes and burned each and every one of them to the ground. They left nothing of the village except piles of ash and old stone chimneys that wouldn't burn. They drove the folk out of their village and into the mountains and warned them against ever coming back to the valley again.

"Oh, for a while, there were still sheep or goats missing, an occasional field burned, but they set guards and beat anyone they found coming near, and before you knew it, the trouble stopped, and the villagers forgot all about the folk they drove out of the valley. It was a sad day for our village, but a sadder day for the other folk. They took to the mountains and vowed to live there with no help from the villagers. They lived in caves and hunted their food. They hated anyone and anything from the valley. My father knew about them and had seen them occasionally, but he kept his distance, and they left him alone. He was the one that told me the stories."

"But, Granny, how long have they been living in the mountains? Are you sure they still live up there?"

"I see them once in a while when I travel there. They are never aware that I am there, so it's easy to watch them. They've changed a lot since they left. They've become quite good at hunting and gathering what food they can. Their caves keep them warm in the winter and cool in the summer. They are a lot like us. They want to be left alone, raise their families, and keep to themselves. They seem to have chosen leaders, as far as I can tell from my travels there. As for how long, Conor, this happened in my grandmother's time, when she was a young girl. No one is still alive that had anything to do with it, but by all accounts, the Mountain Folk still harbor a deep hatred for us lowlanders, as they call us. Which is why I fear for Erik. If they have indeed taken him, it does not bode well for his safety. I want to find him as soon as possible."

Granny set a stiff pace once more, now that her story was told and she could concentrate on walking and breathing. Conor was silent as he walked beside her, thinking of the mistakes made by both sides so many years ago and how it might affect them all today. *The mistakes of our forebears sometimes visit us generations later*, he thought to himself as they walked. Was that fair? Was it right that generations who came after the deed had to pay the price? These thoughts puzzled him as they walked ever higher in search of the Mountain Folk and Erik Tamen.

13

THE MOUNTAIN FOLK

Aelf stood at the edge of his dwelling, a cave with woven branches that created a tight, waterproof door when hung from the top. He stretched his arms high over his head and greeted the sun, as he did every morning. He took a moment to consider his blessings and the day before him. He frowned, thinking of the decision that he must make this day.

A tall man with extraordinary strength, Aelf commanded the attention of everyone when he walked into a gathering or stood to take control of a meeting. Long, brown hair that curled around his shoulders when loose was held back today by a piece of deer hide. His face was brown from hours spent hunting in the sun, his eyes dark gray and always attentive.

At times hotheaded, he often sat alone with his own thoughts, brooding over words spoken in anger. He could be a good listener, someone who would hear out the Folk no matter how long or tedious the story, but impatience sometimes overtook him, and he wished mightily that he could be hunting and not listening to the Folk drone on about problems that seemed trivial and of no concern to him. He never rushed to judgment but would render a judgment that, in the end, everyone agreed with. He had been elected their leader years ago, not a role he sought out but one that he had accepted when it was clear that the Folk were determined.

He was aware of their story, thanks to their healer, Ronan, who was charged, like healers before her, with the job of keeping the stories alive. He was determined from the start that the Folk would work together, raise children together, celebrate together, and support one another. The men would hunt together and share the bounty. The women would gather the fruits, nuts, and seeds from the valleys tucked between the mountains, and all would be shared among the Folk. Men would build shelters; tan the deer, elk, and bear hides for clothing and bedding; and protect the Folk from lowlanders and any other threat. The women would raise the children, caring for them in a community. They would preserve food for the long mountain winters, prepare food to feed everyone, and tend to the sick and infirm, with no regard to which family they belonged. Everything would be shared, the work as well as the bounty. Aelf knew that only in this way could their survival in the mountains be assured. Never again would the Folk depend on outsiders or lowlanders to help them. Self-sufficiency was the key to their survival, and he meant for that to happen now and for the next generation to learn and carry on.

Looking down from the height of his shelter, he could see the women already bustling about the morning meal, one or two children playing among the rocks under the watchful eyes of the Folk, and men sitting quietly, talking and smoking their hand-carved pipes. He knew what they were talking about. The same thing that he must decide, the fate of the lowlander.

From the valley below, the mountains looked simple—straight up to peaks that towered above one another. What you couldn't see from a distance were all the cracks and crevices, the crags, the shelves, and best of all the series of caves created centuries ago. The caves, for the most part, were hidden from the eyes of lowlander hunters behind rock walls that looked as if they extended one to the other, but in fact they overlapped one behind the other, creating the illusion of solid walls. Once a person drew close to them, it was evident that one ended and the other began behind the first. If a hunter were to squeeze between the space, he would discover a world of caves, dwellings built in the tight valleys between the mountains, and a community of people, industrious, self-sufficient, and highly suspicious of any outsider, particularly the people they called lowlanders.

Aelf pushed aside the woven branches that served as a door and entered his cave. He shared this home with his wife, Shaen, and their three boys, Kevin, Brian, and Neall. Shaen was busy boiling water in a gourd set on rocks around a small fire. The smoke from the fire curled up and out through a small hole in the top of the cave. Into the gourd, she poured handfuls of grain and small nuts she had gathered earlier. Using a small, forked stick, she turned pieces of meat on a rock set in the middle of the fire. The meat sizzled as it hit the hot rock, and the smell filled the cave. Wooden dishes sat next to the fire, waiting for the cooked grains and tender pieces of meat. On another rock, she turned over cakes made from seeds and nuts, held together with bear fat. Essential to their well-being, the fat was used sparingly to bind the grains and seeds together. Dried berries were next poured into the gourd of cooked grains, and again, the smell made Aelf's nose tickle with the deliciousness of it.

He sat down on a pile of the softest deer hides piled high in the corner. Nearby were rock ledges with more hides and pillows stuffed with pine needles. Shelves, naturally carved by the forces of nature and some carved out of the rock walls by Aelf, held more dishes and utensils. Stores of grains, nuts, and dried fruit were stacked up on shelves in hopes that mice would not climb that high, a hope never realized. Gourds of precious bear fat were stored on a separate shelf, along with a few ornaments carved from wood and bone. Delicate birds, deer, bears, trees, and flowers carved by Aelf during long winter days were scattered around the cave. Three smaller shelves for sleeping were stacked high with hides, meant for three small boys.

Shaen piled meat in one bowl, cooked grains and fruit in another, and in the third she heaped the small cakes, still steaming from the fire. She poured water into another gourd and handed all of this to Aelf for his morning meal. Serving herself, she sat next to him on the hides and laid her hand on his arm.

"How are you today, my husband?" she asked. "Have you reached a decision?"

He used the small carved spoon to shovel the grains into his mouth to avoid answering her. Chewing thoughtfully, he looked out the doorway to the blue sky and mountain peaks beyond. "Wife, this morning meal is the best I have ever had. You have a way with the simplest food, making it taste delicious." He picked up the slices of meat and smelled them before popping them into his mouth. "I never know what you season this meat with, but you make the toughest meat tender and sweet." He chewed the meat, drinking from the gourd to wash it all down.

She looked at him thoughtfully. "Thank you, dearest. And you have the smoothest way of avoiding a question of anyone I know." She bent her head over her bowl and smiled to herself. She knew him well enough to know that avoiding a question meant that he had no answer, not something that surprised her, considering the decision that he had to make. "Would you like to talk it through, my heart?"

"Ah, Shaen, love of my life. You know me well. And yes, talking it through might help me see it more clearly. On the one hand, it has been our practice for years to avoid lowlanders, and if we came across one, we had two choices. First, make sure they didn't see us. We've hidden from them for years, and although some of them do come up to the mountains, we make sure they can't find our village and our homes. Second, if we cannot possibly avoid them, we deal with them harshly. We let them know they are not welcome, and there have been times when we did that with our bows and arrows, spears, and slings. Not so much in my lifetime, but my da told me many a story of driving lowlanders away from our homes in the past. Over the years, they have come to avoid us as much as we avoid them. But now, we have this man. Clearly, he is a lowlander, and clearly, he has some sort of mission up here. I can't help but wonder, Shaen, if his mission isn't similar to ours. I'm not sure we can afford to treat him badly, only to find out we share a common cause." He paused and looked at his wife sadly.

His gaze was returned with a firm, unwavering look from her clear gray eyes. She placed her worn hand on the side of his face briefly. "I think you might need to talk with Cormac, dear one. Ask your brother's advice. You've done well to listen to him in the past, and he has never given you bad council. He might be able to see things more clearly, since he is not so much in the thick of it as you and I are." These words were spoken tenderly but firmly.

"Hmmm. Yes, you know, I will talk with Cormac. The council members might not like it, but he is the person I trust most, other than you. I'll go right after morning meal." He finished his meal in silence, the comfortable silence that people who have loved each other for many years and shared life's blessings and curses often share. He felt no need to talk further but just enjoyed his time with her, because he knew once he finished speaking with Cormac, his time would not be his own. He looked over at the shelves that held the bedding and possessions of his three boys—their three boys. Empty shelves now, although Shaen kept their bedding clean and neat, in the hopes that the beds would once again hold their children.

In a much smaller cave a short distance away, Cormac shared his morning meal with no one but himself and a stray dog. Cormac honestly could not remember when or how he had come by the dog. He threw the dog some of the meat that he had cooked over his fire. The dog almost looked as if he smiled at Cormac while he ate it.

Cormac resembled Aelf in no way, shape, or form, save that he had the same gray eyes as Aelf, but while his brother's eyes were often flashing with spirit and some degree of anger, Cormac's eyes were thoughtful and kind. While Aelf sometimes reacted impulsively, Cormac was more inclined to study and think about a problem for hours, sometimes days. The balance between the two brothers was a good one; while Aelf could be rash, still he made decisions and stuck to them. Cormac, on the other hand, might think about a problem so long that the problem became a bigger, more insurmountable one. In the end, they needed each other to temper impatience in the one and prod reluctance in the other.

Physically, the brothers could not have been less similar. Aelf towered over most men, one of the reasons the Folk had chosen him to be their leader. Physical strength was prized among the Folk, and Aelf was the best example of that. Cormac, on the other hand, had been slight at birth and never caught up. He was slightly stooped when he walked, and an old injury to his leg caused him to limp slightly. His voice was not the booming voice of Aelf but a soft voice, more like his mother's from years behind him. He lived a solitary life, visiting with Aelf and Shaen and their three boys, the lights of his life.

He sat thinking about them as he ate, remembering how they would come to him straight after morning meal to bedevil him into teaching them some trick or telling them a story. The hours spent together at his cave or in the forests around them were hours spent teaching the boys about nature, the stars, the ways of animals and other creatures of the mountains. He would make up stories to explain the creation of all they saw around them, stories full of mythical animals and people. The boys delighted in their uncle's stories, often begging him to tell another and another until Cormac finally shooed them away and declared that it was time to go hunt mushrooms or wild rice.

Cormac thought of Kevin, the oldest of their three boys, who was most like him. Serious and thoughtful, Kevin took the job of eldest son seriously. A good mix of the two men, he had Aelf's size and strength coming on as he grew but still possessed Cormac's thoughtfulness and compassion. Cormac's lessons were never lost on Kevin, who soaked up the knowledge like dried mushrooms tossed into hot broth.

Brian, the middle child, was the jokester in the family. He loved to play pranks on his brothers, but even more on his mother and father. Hiding his mother's jar of bear fat or taking her favorite cooking tool until she hollered in frustration would make Brian roll on the floor with laughter. If Aelf could not lay his hands on his favorite bow, he had only to look at Brian to find it. Brian's eyes always held a twinkle of amusement, as if he had a secret joke that only he knew. He was the one who most often begged his brothers to go to his uncle's house to hear the stories or learn a new secret of the mountains. He was learning to tell a good story as well as a joke, and that pleased Cormac immensely.

The youngest, Neall, was most like his father. A good boy but sometimes rash, Neall was the boy most likely to get into some kind of trouble from which he needed to be rescued. He was the one who thought he could climb the highest tree, only to become stuck halfway up. His adventures had landed him in more hot water with his father and mother. Try as they might to be angry with him and punish him, one look at his devil-may-care face, and they sighed and let him go off to his next calamity. When the older boys teased him, as older brothers will do, Neall would wade into them with fists flying. Never big enough to do any damage, he received some good beatings, but that never stopped him from trying it again. They often asked him why he kept coming at them, but there was no answer readily available to him except that a feeling overcame him, and he had no choice.

Cormac sat outside his cave and watched his brother, Aelf, approach. "Dog," he said, "it looks like we're in for a long morning. Aelf looks like he could chew the bark off the trees and spit it out again. Better make yourself scarce."

Aelf climbed the path to Cormac's cave and sat down on the pile of hides outside its entrance. He frowned at the dog lying quietly next to Cormac. "You still have that mangy mutt, I see. How much of your meat does he eat, do you suppose?"

Cormac picked up his wooden bowls and utensils to take them into his cave. "Not as much as you think. And what does it matter, Brother? I set enough traps to feed us both." His cave was much smaller than that of Aelf and Shaen. His hides were tanned as smooth and soft as anyone's, and his dishes, carved from some of the most beautiful wood the mountains had to offer, looked as much like works of art as functional items.

He took his time cleaning out his bowls and stacking them on his shelf, straightening the hides on his bed of woven pine branches, taking a broom fashioned from evergreen branches tied onto a shaft and sweeping all the dust and dirt off the cave floor, so that it was as clean and smooth as any woman's home here or in the valley below. Finally, he could delay no more. He knew Aelf needed counsel, but he needed time to think how best to approach the subject.

Aelf sat impatiently outside the cave until Cormac joined him. "I believe you are as fussy about your home as any woman I know, Brother." This was said kindly, for surely, except for Shaen and his children, there was no one he loved more, and in truth, he had loved Cormac longer than anyone.

Cormac smiled and looked out from under the straight brown hair that always hung over his forehead. With no wife to cut his hair or make sure it was combed every day, he often looked more like a ten-year-old boy than a grown man. "Have you noticed that there are more squirrels around this year?" He said this casually, while taking a hand-carved pipe from his pocket and filling the bowl with a pinch of homegrown tobacco. He offered his pouch to Aelf, who took it gratefully. No one grew tobacco on the mountains like Cormac. In fact, no one seemed to grow any at all, except him.

"Hang squirrels. What do I care about squirrels?" Aelf growled, lighting his own pipe with a small twig he stuck in Cormac's fire to catch.

"Well, you might not care, except that Shaen makes one of the best squirrel stews I've ever had. I thought I might set a trap or two and catch some. If I have any luck, I'll bring some over to her. Mayhap we could trade some meat for some of those good berries she has a knack for finding."

"I didn't come here to talk about berries and squirrels, hang it all, Cormac. I need your advice. Honestly, I need your help."

Cormac sighed and puffed on his pipe for a moment. "I know, Aelf. I didn't mean to pester you. Let's talk. Tell me what's on your mind, as if I didn't know already."

"You know we found a lowlander yesterday while we were out hunting. It looked like the fool man tried to climb down the cliff that overlooks Rock Valley. He hit some tree branches on his way down that might have slowed him and saved his life. As it is, he landed between two boulders. Wedged in pretty tight, but we got him out and carried him out the long way. The way he should have gone in the first place, if he knew anything about these mountains. He's alive, but he hasn't woken up. I told the men to take him to Ronan, but I haven't talked to her yet. Thought I'd better come see you first." Aelf leaned back and glared at Cormac, as if daring him to contradict his story.

"I heard something about a lowlander, but I didn't hear the whole story. What's the problem, Aelf? Let Ronan work on him. He either lives or he dies. If he dies, your problem is over; if he lives, send him on his way. I don't see what the problem is, Brother."

"You know the law. No lowlander is allowed to leave our camp. We can't have him going down to the valley and telling them about us. For all they know, we've vanished off the face of the earth, and we need to keep it that way. But Cormac, the man was obviously on a mission. He had a pack with three or four days' worth of food in it. He's not a traveling tinker or a vagrant. His clothes are well cared for, his hair and beard trimmed. I think he's looking for something, and I don't think it is us. He was headed toward The Peak. You know which one I mean. The one with the clouds. What if he's looking for the same thing we've been searching for? What if he's looking for children like we are?"

"We're still sending out search parties, Aelf? Who's out looking now?"

"I have four men out this time: Padrick, Brian, Shawn, and Thomas. They've been gone for two days now."

"Aelf, it's been months since the boys have been gone. And the other children as well. How many have we got left, two or three? Do you really think the children are out there somewhere in these mountains? How do you think they have survived? Aelf, there are wolves, mountain lions, and bears here. How do you think our children are going to be found?" He looked down at the dirt between his feet as he said this, hiding the tears in his eyes.

Aelf shook his head. "As long as I am the leader here, we look for the children. We never give up. My own sons are out there somewhere. I would be out there looking myself if I thought I could do any better than the best trackers we have here. But, Cormac, what if the lowlander is looking for children? What if he knows something that we don't know? Can we take a chance on that?"

"No, you can't. You would never forgive yourself. I think you'd better hope that Ronan can bring him around and he has answers for you. Let the Folk know that you are willing to let Ronan heal him only because he might have answers for us. If he has none, then your job is to get rid of him as quickly as possible."

Aelf ran his hand through his hair and rubbed his eyes. He had never, in all these years, had to decide a man's fate, other than the judgments he rendered over disputes about boundaries and settling the petty arguments that came up when people lived in close proximity to one another. To decide whether a man was valuable to them, valuable enough to keep alive, and if not, then what? Could he afford to let the man go back, with the knowledge of the Folk in the mountains? He already knew the answer to his own question. He didn't need Cormac's advice on that. The law was clear and had been in place for more years than he had been alive. As the leader, he had sworn to uphold those laws, no matter how difficult it might be.

"I'll go see Ronan first, and then I'll call the council to meet. You'll be there?"

Cormac nodded. He would be by his brother's side, the place that he had been for most of his life.

14

THE HEALER AND THE COUNCIL

R onan bent over the man lying on the extra bed in her dwelling. She placed her hand on his forehead to check for fever. She ran her hands down his legs and arms to search for broken bones. Surprisingly, there were none. *I don't know how he managed to fall down that cliff and not break every bone in his body. The fates must favor this man, to keep him from dying then and there.* She checked the bandage wrapped around his head. Blood had seeped through and stained the wool cloth she used.

Hang it all. I don't have much of this left. I'll have to soak it to get the blood out. She quickly and efficiently unwound the strip of wool from around his head and inspected the wound. The back of his head was torn open to the skull all along the back. His hair, what was left, was hanging by skin alone. She cleaned the wound, replaced the skin and hair along his scalp, and wound a clean wool strip around and around his head to hold everything in place. The man was quiet, his eyes closed, his breathing shallow but regular.

Who are you? she wondered to herself. *Besides a lowlander, which only spells trouble for you. I'm surprised they brought you out of the valley at all and doubly surprised they brought you to me. They know as a healer,*

I'm duty bound to do my best for you. Why they didn't just pick up a rock and finish what you started, I'll never know.

She brought broth from her fire and a wooden spoon to slip as much between his lips as she could. Holding his head up so he wouldn't strangle on the broth, she spooned a small bit into his mouth and once again laid his head on the hides. After straightening the hides that covered him and checking to make sure that his breath still left and entered his body, she stepped out into the bright sunshine.

From here she had a view of the forest beyond their village. Her cave was the farthest back, tucked away from everyone else. She had a purpose for this. As the Folk's healer, she often had ill people in her cave for days at a time. She wanted them to be far enough away from the other Folk that there would be peace and quiet. At least, that's the story she'd told the Folk when she chose this out-of-the-way dwelling. In truth, she preferred the quiet location for herself.

Many an evening after her work was done and she had no one to tend to, she would sit outside her dwelling and watch the moon rise and the stars begin to show themselves in the night sky. Being away from the cooking fires meant no light to distract from the nightly show of starlight and moonlight. The quiet in the mornings suited her as well, for she took out leftovers from her evening meal and sprinkled them around her cave. Eating her own meal, she watched the birds, squirrels, and even an occasional deer come to enjoy what she left for them. Too near anyone's cave would mean that hunters would find her habit to their liking, an easy way to gain extra meat for the Folk. It wasn't that she would deny them the food, but she always thought that the few that came to her doorway wouldn't improve anyone's life but hers.

She sat now and waited for the man she knew was coming. Though Ronan had some of the gift of telling, it was not her gift this morning that she used to tell her that Aelf would be coming. She knew the law as well as anyone, and she knew the history and the stories better than most. To keep a lowlander, to allow a lowlander access to their village, was against all the laws that they lived by. The laws were in place to keep them safe, and to flout one was to allow anyone to break any of the laws. Staying together as a community, working, and sharing everything, had been the key to their survival, and to break away from that might mean certain disaster for them all. And yet, what if this man had answers that they needed? What if he knew something they did not know but that was vital in their search for their children? Was that worth breaking the law? She shook her head and thought it was a good thing it wasn't her decision to make.

Ronan sat in the sun, waiting for Aelf to appear. She thought of her last few years as healer for the Folk and everything she had done and the things she was not able to do. You can't live with regrets, but there were things she would have changed if given the power to do so.

She stood and stretched her back, raising her arms high over her shoulders. Ronan was not a tall woman, but there was an erect way she carried herself, with grace and dignity, that made her seem taller than she was. Her brown hair, now streaked with gray, was plaited in one single long braid that hung down her back to her waist. She often pulled it over her shoulder and let it hang there when she was nursing young ones. If they squirmed or fussed, she used the end of it to tickle them under their chin or on their forehead while she hummed to them. There was something quite magical about the combination that soothed any child put in her care. The Folk would stand off to the side, wringing their hands and crying, but as soon as she tickled and hummed to their wee ones, they relaxed as much as the children did.

Ronan had the Folk's knowledge of herbs and remedies, although she feared that much had been lost over the years of isolation in the mountains. She grieved that there were things she could not fix, remedies that she didn't know about that could have made a difference to the Folk at one time or another. While she could brew a tea to help put people to sleep, she didn't know how to take away the pain of childbirth or ease the pain of a broken leg. There was no one to teach her, and that drove her mad some days when they brought her someone with a grievous injury. Like the man inside. He slept, but it was not the sleep of a well man. She could clean his wound and bandage it, but she could not wake him or ease the pain that was hidden inside him. She could poke and probe for broken bones, but what if there was something broken inside that she couldn't see? She shook her head in frustration. *I need someone to help me learn more, someone to teach me. If only I had more knowledge, think of what I might be able to do for my people.*

Aelf rounded the corner and saw Ronan sitting outside, lost in thought. So focused was she that she never heard him approach and was startled by his voice.

"Ronan, you are leagues away in your mind. I swear you did not hear me walk up to you or even call out. What has got you so far away?"

"Aelf, you did startle me. I was thinking of all the things that I don't know."

"Well, if you don't know them, then how can you think about them?" He said this with a chuckle, because he knew exactly what Ronan was talking about. They had this conversation at least once a month. He knew in his heart that Ronan longed to go down to the valley to meet with healers below and learn from them. He also knew that would never happen. The Folk couldn't do without her, even for a short time, and any contact with the lowlanders would be voted down by the council. He regretted that for her and for the Folk. He knew in his heart that the knowledge she could acquire and bring back to them would be of benefit to all.

"What brings you to my door, oh Leader of us all?" Ronan was the one person besides Shaen who could tease Aelf. Such a good heart as hers was never able to be mean to anyone, and Aelf knew that as surely as he knew his name.

"I came to check on the lowlander. How is he today, Healer?"

"He is still sleeping. Not a sound has passed his lips. He has a very ugly wound on the back of his head, and I suspect that's what keeps him asleep. I have felt for broken limbs, but I found none. I wish I could tell what else is going on in his body, but I don't have the skill for that. All I can do is keep his wound clean and give him broth to nourish him." This was said sadly and with regret.

"I see. I'm calling a council meeting for this afternoon, and we'll have to decide what to do with him. This is not a decision I want to make on my own. The council needs to be involved."

"I will tell you this, Aelf, and you take my words to the council. As long as that man is in my care, no harm comes to him, from you or anyone else. I will do everything I can to heal him and send him on his way, but I will be no part of hurting that man. Take my words to the council, Aelf, and mind you tell them with the exact tone that I am using!" Her voice was firm, and her gray eyes shot sparks at him.

"Ronan, I am not in favor of any harm coming to him, but you know the law. At any rate, we would never ask you to carry out a sentence we pass on him. Come to the council meeting, if you wish, and tell them yourself, or I will carry your words to them and make them understand. But Ronan, the law is the law, and we can't change that. Only the council can." He stood up and laid his hand briefly on her shoulder. Giving it a small squeeze of understanding, he turned to walk down the path from her cave.

"Hang it all. I just might go to his blasted council meeting! Someone needs to speak for this man; he surely cannot speak for himself right now." She stood and brushed imaginary crumbs from her skirt and went into the cave to check on her patient.

The council met in a natural amphitheater created by the heaving of mountains and underground plates buried deep within the earth. The walls of the mountain curved around, creating a semicircle of high rocks that stretched to the sky. Within the space, the Folk had carved fallen trees into benches, with several benches up against the rock wall and even more placed in a half circle some distance from them. When the council met, they would hear arguments or petitions from the Folk and carry on their own discussions and disagreements right in front of their audience. No one wanted any discussion to occur in private; everything needed to be in front of everyone. That was the law. The Folk believed that secret-keeping was one of the many things that had led to their banishment from the valley, and like with sharing and being self-reliant, they were determined that the old habits would be replaced with new ones.

The council members filed in first and took their seats facing the many carved benches. Aelf joined them and sat at the very end, not in the middle. It was not his job to run the council meetings. That was a shared responsibility that rotated among the members. His voice would carry no more weight when it came time to make a decision than anyone's voice. If there was ever a time when his voice seemed to carry such weight, it was only because the council was inclined to listen more carefully to him. He was, after all, their leader, but more than that, they knew him to be a man who made sound, reasonable decisions.

The council consisted of nine members: five women and four men. The Folk cast ballots once a year to elect the members, and every other year, the balance between men and women would shift. Anyone could run for council positions; age did not matter to the Folk. Reasonableness, sound judgment, and a willingness to listen to all sides involved meant the most to them, and this year's council reflected that. Two of the women were gray-haired and wrinkled, while the other three were young, some barely married. Of the four men, Aelf represented the middle age, with two of the men older than he and one much younger. The Folk found that too many very old voices could get lost in reflection and think too much of the way things had been in the past, while too many young people were ready to change too much too quickly. Balance in everything, they thought, served them best. And so today, a balance of the old laws and a new need would come head-to-head in debate and a final vote.

Any one of the Folk could bring a problem or a dispute before the council, with the understanding that whatever the council decided would bind both parties. No arguments were put forth once the council voted on a matter. The subject was closed, and it then became the job of Aelf to see that the judgment was carried out by all parties concerned. Over the years, Aelf was given the job of enforcing boundaries, distributing food and tools fairly, supervising the sharing of belongings of Folk taken from this world, and even the banishment of Folk who had committed the ultimate crime, that of taking a life. He was prepared to carry out the wishes of the council, whatever they decided about the lowlander, but his hope was that it would be a decision that he could live with.

The rest of the Folk filed in and took places on the benches facing the council. Cormac and Ronan entered together and sat beside each other. The Folk whispered among themselves until one of the council, Maeve, with her long gray hair and a map of wrinkles across her face, stood and rapped her long staff on the ground sharply, calling the council meeting to order.

"Is there any business to bring before the council?" she asked of the Folk. All were quiet then, waiting for someone to bring up the problem of the lowlander.

A woman stood up at the back of the room and said, "I have a problem to bring before the council."

"Come forward, then, and say your piece." Maeve sat back down at her place while the woman came forward.

The woman stepped forward and began a long story of a neighbor who had borrowed bowls and utensils and failed to return them promptly. When reminded, the woman gave them back in disrepair or broken altogether. Maeve called the accused woman forward to hear her side of the story. She claimed the items had been lent in that condition, and she used them and gave them back as soon as she could. People fidgeted on their benches, impatient with the two women and their squabble over bowls and serving forks. The council members asked clarifying questions to try to determine the facts. After hearing the women, they talked it out among themselves, allowing their audience to hear every word spoken.

Finally, Maeve called for a decision, and one was rendered: the woman did indeed borrow the dishes in question and kept them too long. She returned them in less good order than she had borrowed them in. Their decision: she must take back the broken items and replace them with items that were carved by the best carver in the village. She would have to pay for them with skins or gathered food, it was her choice. She would have until the next full moon to fulfill the judgment, and Aelf would see to it that she did.

The Folk nodded their heads in agreement. It was a fair decision.

Everyone knew the woman borrowed everything from everyone, and her returning things was often in question. Most often, people forgot they had lent her things, or they just didn't think it was worth bothering, but finally someone had had enough, and now the woman would learn a lesson.

The people shifted impatiently in their seats, whispered to one another, and watched the council members anxiously. Everyone knew there was something important afoot, but the rumors had been flying for over a day now, and the story was a little hard to untangle. They peered over their shoulders at Ronan and Cormac, who sat in the back of the space, their heads together, whispering to one another.

At last, the council asked if there was any more business they needed to hear before discussion began on the topic of the day. The Folk stared at one another, daring anyone to have another problem that took up time and energy. No one moved from the benches, so with a sigh, the council leader stood and rapped her staff three times on the ground.

"We have a problem that has come before us. This is a problem that we've had before and knew exactly how to handle, but circumstances have changed, and we must now consider those changes before we make a decision. The first person we want to hear from is Ronan."

Ronan shook her head and left the bench she shared with Cormac. Walking forward, she stood in front of the council.

"Tell us about the lowlander, Ronan."

The Folk gasped and immediately began whispering among themselves. So it was true, there was a lowlander among them. How had this person come to be in their village? Why was he here? What would the council do with him?

"He's badly injured, Maeve. He has an injury to the back of his head that is quite severe. I cannot tell if he has any additional broken bones, but I don't think he does. I have run my hands over his limbs and feel nothing out of the ordinary, although I cannot figure out how he could fall that far and not have broken every bone in his body. He might have injuries inside him, but this I cannot tell, because I don't have the knowledge that helps me discover so. He sleeps at present. I bathed his wound yesterday when the men brought him to me and again this morning. I give him broth, a few sips at a time, as many times as I can get him to swallow. He has a bad wound, but I have seen worse. I'm not sure if it is the wound that keeps him asleep or something else. Again, I do not have enough knowledge to be able to determine this." Ronan stated all of this in a flat voice, with no drama or emotion. Then she stood silently, waiting for questions from the council.

The council put their heads together and murmured for a moment. One of the members, a tall, thin man with an ever-present frown on his face, rose and asked, "I understand that he sleeps, Ronan, but has he said anything in his sleep?"

"No, Daniel, no words have passed his lips that I have heard."

"Thank you. I don't think we have any more questions for you. We want you to keep him alive the best you can, Ronan, until we tell you otherwise."

"Daniel, I need to say one more thing. I know the law as well as anyone. But you need to understand that I am a healer, and that means I can never do anything to harm a person. It is the vow I took when I started my journey as a healer. If the council decides that he must die, it will not be by my hand."

"Ronan, we are aware of your oath as a healer, and we would never ask you to do anything against that oath. Thank you. That will be all."

Maeve rose from her seat and addressed the Folk, "Is there anyone here who would like to speak on behalf of the lowlander?"

Aelf rose from his seat and walked around to stand in front of the council. "I would, Maeve. I would like to address the council and the Folk." He turned to face them.

"I know the law. I uphold the law; that's the job you gave me years ago. I would never knowingly break any law of the Folk, but today I am here to plead for a change. You all know what we have suffered the last few months. First one child, and then another, disappeared from our homes, our village. You know Shaen and I have lost all three of our sons, but I know some of you have lost that many and more. Those who still have children are frantic with worry that their children might be next. You hold on to them so tightly that they can barely breathe.

"You know I have tracked the children, and some of our best trackers have scoured these mountains looking for signs of our children. We've considered wild animals, maybe lions or bears. We've doubted and suspected each other and turned against one another until we realized we must work together. But try as we might, we just keep running into a stone wall. Our grief is so deep that I wonder some days how we go about the job of keeping the village going. If it were not that our elders need to eat and the remaining children need to be cared for, I wonder that we would not have just picked up and moved on. I know all of this, and yet, I have been helpless to make any difference. No matter what I've done, the result is the same; our children are gone, and we just can't find them.

"But then a lowlander comes up to the mountains, obviously looking for something. He has enough supplies in his pack for a few days. So, I ask myself, what is he looking for? He's not a hunter. While he had a good knife at his belt, his bow and arrows were suited for small game, not deer or bear. So what is he doing here, I ask myself? Perhaps he is looking for the same thing we are looking for—children! What if we are not the only ones who have lost children these last few months? What if the lowlanders have also lost children? What if many lowlander villages have lost children?

"What I am asking the council to agree to is this: allow Ronan to do her job with this man. If he wakes up, let us question him before we deal with him by the law. Let us find out if he has common cause with us. Perhaps he knows something that we don't know. That is all I ask of the council." Aelf looked back at Cormac, who nodded to his brother. Aelf took his place once again with the council.

The council looked at one another and then at the Folk, all leaning toward them with breath held. Maeve rose once again and rapped her staff on the floor, a meaningless gesture, since there was not a sound in the amphitheater. Everyone held their breath and waited. "Is there anyone else who would like to speak?" She asked the Folk. There was one huge intake of breath, as if someone had commanded the Folk to breathe all at the same time. Hands shot up immediately. Maeve took an involuntary step backward. "Let me ask this in another way," she said gently. "Is there anyone here who would like to speak in favor of Aelf's request?" Again, half the hands in the group shot up immediately. There were some who raised their hands more slowly, but at the end of a breath or two, every hand in the group was raised. Every face was determined, and some looked as fierce as if they were being challenged by last year's rogue bear.

Maeve smiled at the Folk. "There are Folk here that I know have lost children. I expected them to speak, but there are others of you who have no children or, better still, yet have theirs tucked safely away." She turned to face the council. "We can talk this through if you want. That is the rule, and I am certainly willing to abide by it, but it looks to me as if we have the clear voice of the Folk, and it is our duty to listen to them and carry out their wishes. Do you all agree?"

Every council member looked sadly at the Folk, still with their hands raised high. Some had left their seats and were standing, some with tears in their eyes, some with scowls, as if they expected an argument. The council members each, in turn, nodded in the affirmative, and thus it was passed. Ronan would do everything in her power to heal Erik Tamen, and then they would see if he sought the same thing they searched for so desperately—the missing children.

15

UNWELCOME GUESTS

Granny, Conor, and Wolf spent the night under the spreading branches of a giant fir tree. Crawling beneath the branches that swept the ground, they were hidden from anyone or anything that might chance too close to them. Their evening meal was eaten cold to avoid a fire that might alert someone or something to their presence. They gathered up the fir needles, heaping them into piles to make as comfortable a bed as possible, and, wrapping their cloaks around them, lay down to sleep.

In the early morning light, Granny crawled from beneath the branches and found small sticks to make a fire. Taking a flint from her pack, she struck rocks with it until sparks ignited a pile of shredded bark she had laid on top. Blowing gently, she encouraged the sparks to become small flames, then larger ones, as the fire greedily ate at the sticks she had piled together. She fed the fire all she had, watching it burn down to good, hot coals. She found a flat rock, and placing it near the fire, she set two metal cups full of spring water on it. Before too long, the water began to steam, and Granny sifted herbs into the water to make tea. She took out cheese and eggs carefully wrapped in wool. The dried apples and mutton she saved for the midday meal, if they had time to stop and eat. She hoped they would be able to find the Mountain Folk before the sun set, but there were no guarantees.

Granny sipped her tea, fed some of the cheese and bread to Wolf, and waited for Conor to emerge from under the fir branches. When he finally crawled out, fir needles and sticks stuck in his hair and clothing. Granny chuckled when she saw him. *What a ragamuffin he is!*

She handed him the cup of tea and bread and cheese. He squatted down next to her and ate and drank gratefully. The sun was just topping the farthest peak, and the forest looked green and gold in the morning light. Birds were beginning their morning song, and Granny threw some breadcrumbs on the ground to entice them closer. Wolf watched every bit she threw out, until finally he caught Granny's eye.

"You're right, Wolf, you need it far more than even the birds do. We have a long way to travel today, I reckon." She threw the last piece of bread to him, and he caught it and swallowed it in one big gulp. He wandered over to the nearby spring to drink his fill of the fresh water, while Conor finished his breakfast and handed the cup back to Granny to pack away. She sorted through the herbs and ointments in her pack, making sure for the tenth time that everything was in good order.

"Do you think we'll be able to find the Mountain Folk today, Granny?" Conor asked.

"I believe so. I'd like to take a minute to travel before we head out, if you don't mind. It would be nice to know where they are, if that's possible."

Conor nodded and, standing to stretch, whistled to Wolf, and they set out for a look around. Granny settled back and let her mind travel around the mountains. By setting her intentions to find the Mountain Folk, she hoped the journey would be a short and fulfilling one. Her mind took her to a small valley tucked between the mountains. There she stared up at a wall of rock that looked like a dead end. Her mind was still, and she waited for what she might find there. Sure enough, within a few minutes, she sensed movement and voices behind the wall. Setting herself out in the direction of the sounds, she realized that the wall was an illusion. Where the first wall stopped, almost immediately a second wall behind it began, making it seem as if it were one continuous wall. *Oh, how clever these Mountain Folk are,* she thought to herself. Squeezing between the two rocks, she traveled in her mind up the path and around a bend, where before her mind's eye she saw a warren of caves and a beehive of activity. She quickly noted where the two walls were in relation to the rest of the mountains and then let her mind slip back to her body.

Conor and Wolf had returned from their scouting trip and sat watching her from under a nearby tree. "Did you find them?" he asked.

"Yes, they are some distance from here, but not so far that we can't make it before dark, I think. That is, if we leave right now. There will be a little climbing involved. Your strong legs will have to help my poor old legs up some of the way, but between you and Wolf, we'll get there." She picked up her walking stick, settled her pack across her shoulders, and set out, with Conor and Wolf behind.

Granny set a fast pace, not stopping for midday meal, steadily climbing up and across the valleys and smaller peaks. Conor thought to ask her to stop and allow him to catch his breath and then realized how silly that would seem. Ask an ancient woman to let him rest? Cripes! What happened to her old, tired legs needing help, he could never tell.

As the sun began to sink below the mountains, Granny led Conor and Wolf to the wall. She sat down and took out a water bag to drink. She passed it to Conor, who drank gratefully. "I didn't think you were ever going to stop, Granny. I thought you said you might need some help getting up the trail. It looks to me like you could outwalk me and Wolf with little trouble." He grinned at her and took another drink from the water bag. Passing the bag back to her, he asked, "This looks like a dead end, Granny. Where do we go from here?"

"It just looks like that, Conor. I thought the same thing when I traveled here this morning, but I soon realized just how clever the Mountain Folk have become. The wall in front ends and another begins, but from here it looks like one long, tall wall. There is a narrow space we can use to get to their village. I want to wait a minute and put our heads together to come up with a plan. I'm afraid if we just go marching into their village like we belong there, our welcome might be less than we want it to be."

Granny took her walking stick and began to draw circles in the dirt in front of their feet. Conor watched and waited. He knew that Granny needed time to sort things out in her mind before she would offer a plan. He also knew enough to be quiet and let her work it out. When she was ready, they would talk. He settled back against a rock and absentmindedly petted Wolf's ruff along his neck.

At last Granny raised her face up and stopped drawing circles. "I think the best plan would be to walk into their village with our hands raised so that they see we have no weapons, nothing threatening. I doubt the welcome will be good, but perhaps they will give us a chance to talk before they take any action. I thought of pretending that you were injured and we needed help, but I don't want to start out with a lie. They need to trust us, and a lie is the best way to make sure that never happens. Can you put a rope around Wolf so he is less threatening? I know you trust him, and so do I, but again, they won't, and I don't want anything to happen to your dog, or us. What do you think, Conor?"

Conor shook his head. "I don't know what to expect, Granny. If they have Erik Tamen, do you think they may harm him if they feel we are a threat to them?"

"I don't know, Conor. I didn't take the time to go into their village and find him. To be honest, I sensed something there that made me reluctant to go in."

Conor waited for her to explain.

"I felt as if someone knew that I was there. It's not a feeling I get very often. There aren't many travelers that I know about, and certainly I never heard that any of the Mountain Folk could travel, but mark my words, someone in that village knows how to travel, even if they don't realize it."

One last time, they picked up their packs and sticks. Conor took a short length of rope from his pack and tied it around Wolf's neck. Wolf looked indignant at the very idea of being leashed, but Conor patted his head and assured him it was for his own good. Together, in single file, they walked to the end of the rock wall and found the opening between the two rocks. With Granny leading the way, they walked toward the Mountain Folk village. Squeezing through the opening, they came into a perfect clearing of green grass and wildflowers. A short distance away, they could see the caves that dotted the face of the next set of peaks. They stood quietly and observed the women working together to fix the evening meal, men tanning hides or carving bowls from wood, and children sitting quietly together under a nearby tree.

Just then, one of the village dogs raised its head and howled a warning to the Mountain Folk. Everyone froze, turning to see what had the dog alarmed. Quickly, with no wasted movement, some of the women gathered the children and carried them back to the cooking fires. The men grabbed up spears or bows and arrows and rushed toward Granny and Conor. They both raised their hands high and stood their ground, though it was difficult when faced with charging men with spears. Before you could take two breaths, the men surrounded the three weary travelers, pointing spears or notched arrows in bows.

16

AELF MEETS HIS MATCH

Wolf's hackles were raised, and a low growl rose from his throat. Conor gave a gentle tug on the rope around his neck and urged him to be quiet. He and Granny stood still with arms held high to show that they had no weapons and were no threat to the Folk. One of the men gestured for them to follow him, and when they fell in behind him, the rest of the men followed on three sides, still holding their weapons trained on the two. Conor felt a little like giggling for a brief second. Did these men really think that he and Granny presented any kind of danger to the Folk? He just as quickly stifled the urge. *No sense making men with spears mad, right?*

The man led them up the path to the collection of caves in the mountainside. They walked past what looked to Conor like a huge, hollowed-out space, with benches all facing one row of seats in the front. *What could that be for?* he wondered. They climbed a path leading to a cave with a screen of woven branches. Once outside, the man called out, "Shaen, is he within? Is your husband here? See what we've found."

A tall man pulled the woven branches aside and stepped out. Immediately, Conor thought he was the largest man, save Erik Tamen, that he had ever seen. The man wore soft deer hide pants and a shirt made of woven bark that looked as soft as any cloth made by the women of his own village. The man's long hair curled around his shoulders, but it was his eyes that held Conor's attention. Dark gray, they were the most direct eyes he'd ever seen, as if the man could look right into his heart and tell him what kind of person he was.

"What the devil do you have here, Daniel?" he asked.

"They came walking into our village. Hands held up. Leading this dog behind them. This can't be a coincidence, right? This has to be about the lowlander. We thought we'd better bring them to you to figure out what to do with them." Daniel lowered his spear and, with one last look at Granny, walked away down the path.

Aelf sighed and ran his hands through his hair, pulling it away from his face. *Just like Erik Tamen,* Conor thought.

"All right, come in and sit down. You don't look like much of a threat to me, but keep that dog on his rope, do you hear?"

Conor nodded, and he and Granny followed Aelf into the cave. "Sit!" Aelf gestured to a pile of hides on a shelf. "Shaen, we have visitors. Would you bring tea, please?"

He sat opposite them and stared without saying a word. Under such an intense stare, Conor began to fidget, getting increasingly nervous. Granny sat still and quiet, as calm as if she were having a cup of tea on her front porch. The woman he called Shaen came from the back of the cave and looked with astonishment at the three of them sitting in her home. "I see we are to be completely overrun with lowlanders, my dear. Tea, you say. Will they be here long enough to drink it?"

Aelf grinned at the woman, leaving Conor to gape at them both. He seemed so angry, so serious, and yet, here this woman was teasing him as if they both shared a joke. She began to pour water into a gourd and set it by the fire that held the morning ashes. Piling small sticks and shredded bark on the coals, she blew gently until flames began licking at the rock that held the gourd. Before long, but what seemed like an eternity to Conor, she poured four cups of tea and handed them out, keeping one for herself.

"Well, let's hear it. Who are you and what are you doing here?" the man demanded.

Granny sipped her tea for a moment and then smiled at the woman. "Lavender and wheat grass?" she asked. "It's delicious!"

Shaen smiled back at her, thinking that, just perhaps, Aelf might have met his match in this diminutive, gray-haired woman sitting across from them.

"Never mind the tea," he growled. "I want to hear the story now."

Granny continued to sip her tea without the least bit of nervousness. When she finally finished it, she set the cup on the ground beside her and, looking at the woman, said, "Thank you. That was lovely. We've traveled a long way, and a cup of tea was just the thing to settle our nerves."

Shaen chuckled. *There's something about this little woman that just makes your heart happy,* she thought. *The fates better help Aelf when it comes to dealing with this one. He is going to be over his head before he can take a good breath.*

"Enough!" Aelf roared, causing Conor to flinch and Granny to blink once or twice. "I want to know who you are and how you came to be here! How did you find us?"

Granny turned her attention fully on Aelf. "I won't answer your second question, but I will fully explain who we are and what we need. My name is Matilda, and this is Conor. Wolf is his dog. We've come up from the valley looking for a man, and I think you might know something about him. He's a big man, with red hair and beard, and I think he might be injured. I think you have him here in your village. I'd like to see him, please. I know you have a healer here, but I might be able to help him as well." This was all said calmly and quietly but very firmly.

Aelf scowled. "You seem to know an awful lot about us, and I already figured you were a lowlander, you and the boy. You've not come near to answering enough questions to get anything from me." He leaned back and crossed his arms over his chest and stared Granny in the eye.

"Somehow I knew you were going to be difficult. Just answer me, do you have an injured 'lowlander,' as you call us?"

Shaen nodded, earning her a frown from Aelf.

"I thought as much. His name is Erik Tamen, and he's our mayor and constable. He came to the mountains looking for children, our children. We've been losing children for the last few months, one at a time, until there are nearly none left to us."

Aelf's gaze softened, and he, too, nodded. "We've lost nearly all our children. It started almost a year ago and went on for months. We set guards, we've sent out scouts, we've searched the mountains, but we've never found a trace of them. No bodies, no bones, no children. Nothing!"

"I'm sorry, Aelf. I didn't know, but I suspected as much. May I see Erik Tamen now, please?"

"You're a long way from answering my questions, Matilda. I want to know how you know about us, and for that matter, how do you know my name? I don't recall giving it to you, nor anyone calling me by name since you've been here."

"I promise, I will answer all your questions, but first I must see the man. I need to see what your healer is doing for him and if there is anything I can do to assist her."

"How did you know our healer was a woman?"

Granny's look was steady and patient, but no more would she say. She had the look of a woman who'd caught Aelf snitching a piece of her apple pie and was waiting for an explanation. Her eyebrows raised slightly, and she continued to stare, saying nothing.

"Hang it all! I'll take you to him!" Aelf rose, and with one smooth movement that belied her age, Granny stood and took up her walking stick. Conor gave a tug on the rope around Wolf's neck to get him up. "Do you think it would be all right if I took the rope off Wolf? He's a good dog. He won't fight with your dogs or give you any trouble."

"Mind he doesn't! But yes, go ahead and untie him. He looks like a good dog."

Aelf left the cave, with the three of them close behind. At the last minute, Shaen shook her head and said, "Hang them all. I'll not be left out of this encounter." She, too, followed out of the cave and down the path toward Ronan's dwelling.

Single file, they made their way to Ronan's cave at the very back of the village. Aelf called out once they were there for permission to enter.

Interesting, Granny thought. *He does have manners after all. That's a good thing to know.*

Ronan swept aside the fine piece of woven wool that served as her door and met the group with an astonished look. "What, in all that the fates have called, do you have here, Aelf?" She looked first at Granny, then Conor, and lastly took a long look at Wolf, smiling when she did.

"More lowlanders, Ronan. I believe we're being overrun with them. But true enough, I believe they are looking for the very thing that we're looking for. This is Matilda." He waved his hand at Granny. "She wants to see the man that you're looking after. She thinks she might be able to help you."

Ronan fixed Granny with her gray eyes, and Granny returned the look without wavering. "So, you're a healer, Matilda? I could use some advice. He is still sleeping from a head wound he received when he fell down the cliff. I've been tending to the wound, and it looks like it's healing, but he still sleeps. I can't find any other injuries, but I fear I lack the skill to know whether he has any or not. I welcome the help, Matilda!"

She turned and went back into the cave with Granny behind her. Aelf indicated to Conor that he should stay outside, he and Wolf, with him and Shaen. They found benches made from old logs and settled down. Aelf immediately gave his full attention to Conor. What he saw did not impress him much: a scrawny boy, undersized by the look of him, not well-fed. Brown hair that fell over his forehead and into his eyes, not much really to see, he thought. "How did you come to be up here?" he asked.

Conor brushed the hair out of his eyes and looked directly at Aelf. *I won't budge,* he thought. *He might think he's frightening, but he doesn't scare me one bit.* "We were following Erik Tamen, but we were delayed by a day, so he got a good head start. Granny knew he'd been injured and that you people had him here. She was scared you would harm him, knowing how you feel about lowlanders, as you call us. So we came here as quickly as we could to make sure he was treated well."

Aelf reared back and looked again at this slight boy who spoke with such confidence. "Hang it all, how did she know he was here? That's what puzzles me, boy! I want to know how she knew this!"

"My name is Conor, not boy! When Granny is ready to tell you, she will. Until then, you get nothing more from me." Conor settled back against the wall, put his hand on Wolf's neck, and closed his eyes.

Aelf chuckled. *Well, he might be scrawny, but he's got nerve,* he thought. He looked at Shaen, who smiled at him. *Yes, he reminds me of our son as well,* Aelf thought.

Granny's eyes adjusted to the dim light inside Ronan's cave, and she watched Erik, his chest rising and falling with every breath, eyes flickering behind the lids as if he dreamed. She walked quickly to him and, putting aside the furs covering him, felt his body, poking him in his belly and abdomen, feeling his limbs, and resting her hand on his forehead. "Let me see the wound, please."

Ronan rolled Erik onto his side and thrust a rolled-up hide behind his back to keep him in position. Granny nodded her approval at this technique for holding the patient from rolling back while attending to the wound. Ronan unwound the long strip of wool, rolling it up as she did to make it easier to put back on when they finished examining him. Granny bent close to the wound. Searching for any sign of infection, she put her nose nearly on top of it and smelled deeply. She sat back on her heels and smiled at Ronan. "You've done an excellent job of cleaning and caring for this wound. The scalp will reattach, and no doubt his hair will even grow back. Good thing, too. Erik is quite fond of his thatch of red hair! I smell no sign of infection, which is excellent as well. You're a good healer, Ronan."

Ronan felt her heart swell with the words of praise, but she still frowned. "I can't wake him, Matilda. He has been sleeping ever since they found him, and he has not woken once since they brought him to me. That worries me. I fear there is something broken inside him, and I don't know how to find or fix it." Her frustration was evident to Granny.

"No, my dear. There are no internal injuries, as near as I can tell. You put your hands on him like this. Let me show you." They moved the roll of fur out from behind him and gently put him on his back. Granny pulled the hides back and showed Ronan how she put her right hand flat on him with her left hand over it. Gently, she applied pressure to his stomach, his intestines, and all around his abdomen. All the while, she kept her eyes glued to his face, which never changed. "Do you see how I apply even but firm pressure on all the parts of him that hold his organs? His stomach, his liver and kidneys, his guts? All the while, I watch his face. Even in sleep, if there is something amiss, his face will betray it. There will be a groan, a flinch, an intake of breath. You'll know it when you see it. But, you see, he sleeps peacefully. No, he has no injuries to the inside of him. I think, Ronan, that the injury to his head was so traumatic that he needs to sleep to heal. Our bodies are wiser than we think. They know that to heal means to lie still and be quiet, and in sleep we do that best. Are you feeding him anything?"

"Yes, broth, but he only takes a tiny bit at a time."

"Good, let's keep that up, but I am also going to brew some tea for him that will help with pain. He's bound to have a tremendous headache, and in sleep his body is able to deal with it better. If I can ease that pain, he might allow himself to awaken. There is no promise, but we'll see. Show me how you boil water for tea, please?"

Ronan built up her fire and placed the flat rocks almost within the flames. She filled an earthen pot with water and set it on the rock to boil. Granny nodded her approval, and when the water was steaming, she sifted through her pack until she found the combination of herbs she was looking for. Sprinkling some in the water, she sat back to allow the tea to steep and become strong enough to work its good medicine. She filled the cup that Ronan handed her and, lifting Erik's head, slipped the rolled hide beneath his neck and head.

Slowly, she spooned the tea into his mouth, patiently waiting for him to swallow before she tried another spoonful. In this way, she managed to get the entire cup of tea down his throat. "He will sleep even deeper than before with the tea, but when it begins to ease his pain, he just might wake up. We'll see. Ronan, thank you for looking after him. You've done a fine job. I could have done no better for him."

Ronan smiled at the praise. "How is it that you found us?" she asked.

Granny sighed. "I promised I would tell Aelf the story, but I'm just not in the mood for his glares and growls right this moment. I'm a traveler, Ronan. I have traveled through these mountains in my mind while my poor, tired body stays at home and rests. It's something that I have been able to do since I was a child. I suspect that you are a traveler as well, but I'm not sure you even know it."

Ronan stared, her mouth half-open. "A traveler, you say? You mean you can see things without actually being there in your body? Can you tell things that will happen as well?"

"Yes, and right now I can tell that I would like a cup of tea, please. Shaen was kind enough to give us one earlier, but another would put me right, and I do have a lot to tell you. Tea makes me talkative," she said with a glint in her eye and a smile on her lips.

Ronan blushed. "Forgive my ill manners, Matilda. I should have offered you tea as soon as we finished examining the man. What did you say his name was?"

She bustled about the cave, fixing tea for Granny and some for the visitors outside. After she took cups to Aelf, Shaen, and Conor, she settled down to hear the whole story from Granny.

Granny accepted the cup of tea gratefully but looked at Ronan with worry. "I would love to tell you everything, but the truth is, I promised Aelf I would answer all of his questions. I think I owe him that before you and I talk any further. I would hope that he would allow you to be a part of the conversation. I hope you understand, Ronan. I believe I am going to need his help, your help, all of you, before this is over. That means that I must be as honest with him as I can possibly be to earn his trust. In truth, I will need to earn the trust of all the Mountain Folk, I'm afraid."

Ronan answered, patting Granny on the arm, "You have mine, Matilda, for what it's worth. Let's just enjoy the quiet of a cup of tea and then go poke the bear a little."

17

COMMON CAUSE

Ronan and Granny checked Erik's breathing one more time and then lifted the woven wool blanket and joined Aelf and the others outside.

"About time," he growled. "I thought maybe you were fixing a feast to feed us all, you took so long."

"Oh, Aelf, Matilda was showing me how to examine the lowlander. We fixed tea to help him sleep and heal. I have no idea why I am explaining myself to you. As the healer for the Folk, I have certain privileges, and one of them is the lack of any need to explain myself. To you or anyone! Kindly remember that in the future."

Granny ducked her head to hide her smile, but Conor was not so successful. The chuckle that erupted from his throat was quickly disguised by a cough that fooled no one.

"Hmmph! Are you ready to give me some answers now, Matilda, or whoever you are?"

"Yes, but let us go somewhere comfortable where we won't disturb Erik. He needs his sleep if he is to heal." With that, Granny strode off, as if she knew exactly where she was going. This time, Conor didn't even pretend to hide his laughter. He looked Aelf right in the eyes and laughed out loud. "Guess you better follow her if you want any answers," he said as soon as he could talk without laughing.

Aelf frowned but headed after Granny, and the rest filed in behind him. Conor rubbed Wolf's ears. "I do like the way she treats that man, Wolf. He's a little too big for his own sake, and ours too, I think."

Granny somehow found her way back to Aelf's dwelling and made herself comfortable on a bench outside. Shaen preferred to cook and eat outside in better weather, and Aelf had accommodated her by making something of an outdoor kitchen, with a firepit complete with a stone oven built above it. In good weather, she could be outside to grind the nuts and seeds she gathered. These she mixed with dried fruit and bear fat to make the cakes that were the envy of all the Mountain Folk women.

The other women envied her baking oven, and she took a lot of pride in it, not only for the cakes but for the fact that Aelf would build it for her. In her mind, there was no greater act of love than that, save perhaps for the three strong boys he'd given her. Boys that were now lost to them, or so she'd thought. The words that Granny brought gave her hope that their boys might still walk this earth somewhere—somewhere they could be found. She settled herself on a bench to listen to Granny's words.

"It started just a few months ago, as I told you. One morning, we all heard the most awful wailing imaginable. We rushed to the cottage from where it came and found a mother shrieking that her child was gone. Of course, we all turned out immediately to search the fields, streams, barns, and everywhere we could think. We turned the village upside down, and then, when the child was still lost, we began searching cottages. First the ones nearby, but in the end, every cottage was searched. We found nothing. No trace of the child at all. No scrap of cloth, no dropped doll or toy, no hair ribbon, nothing.

"We widened our search to include the forest beyond the fields. We all carried sticks and beat the bushes, thrust them into holes, swept aside the tall grass. We found no trace. We wept with the parents and tried to console them, but there was no consolation to be had. Two days later, another child disappeared, and we did the same thing all over again. We set guards outside cottages, and fathers stayed awake beside their children, but still the children disappeared. We stopped up the windows with wax, thinking that if a window had been opened, we would see the broken wax, but the next morning the child would be gone, and the wax would be unbroken. We hammered shut doors and stopped up chimneys in fair weather and in foul, built fires high. Everything we did was for nothing. One after another, every few days, a child would be gone. Until at last, my granddaughter, Tilly, disappeared. I left the village shortly after, so I don't know if any other children have disappeared since Tilly."

Aelf frowned at Granny. "This sounds almost exactly like what happened to us, save we had no doors or windows to bar or shut. We set guards as well. We've sent search parties, as I said, but we have found no trace of our children. Shaen and I lost all three of our boys." He hung his head and looked at his hands, which hung uselessly in front of him.

"There's more, please. I told Ronan this, but I knew you deserved to hear the rest of it first. Aelf, I have a gift that is sometimes more of a curse than a gift. Since I was young, I have been able to see what the future holds for some people. I call it 'a telling,' for lack of a better word. Not for everyone and not for everything, but for most people if I set my mind to it. I learned early on that most people don't want to hear what the future holds for them, most particularly if it is bad tidings. Erik is one of those people. I once shared a telling I had for his baby boy, thinking that we could head it off, change the future the fates had for the wee one. It didn't happen, and the boy died as I predicted. Erik never forgave me, as if my telling made it so. I don't believe that to be true. I believe we are in charge of our lives, and if we know something, then we have it within our power to make choices that will change the course of events. Sadly, I am alone in my thinking." Granny said the last with a hint of tears in her eyes, as if the memory were still painful after all these years.

"There is more. I am able to travel through the space around us without my body actually doing it. When my granny found out that I had the gift of telling, she began to work with me to discover what other gifts I might have. She taught me to empty my mind of all thoughts and then fill it with the place that I wished to see. It took me years, but I eventually learned to travel in my mind to almost anywhere I wish. I first heard of you from my dear father, who hunted all over these mountains. And then I found the Mountain Folk village years ago when I wandered these mountains while sitting alone by my fire. I watched you be elected leader. I saw Ronan learn how to be a healer. I've watched your Folk thrive here in the mountains as you never did in the valley. Once I found you, it became a habit to visit you every now and then to see what new things were taking place. But I hadn't come for a very long time, so I didn't know about your children. I wish I had known. We might have helped each other much sooner."

Aelf, Shaen, and Ronan were still and quiet as Granny told her story. Aelf looked at Shaen at the end and shook his head. "What a mistake we've made all these years, shunning the lowlanders and keeping to ourselves."

Shaen patted his hand. "Don't think that, dearest. I have a feeling that Matilda has more to tell us. Something that will lighten our hearts. Is that not so, Matilda?"

Granny nodded. "You might have the gift of telling as well, Shaen. Yes, there is more to tell. I've been watching one of the mountain peaks for the longest time, and I noticed some particular clouds there. Dark clouds that swirl around and around its peak but never blow away. I became convinced that there was something going on there that I needed to know about. So I traveled, and I found a cave, much like your caves here but taller and far wider. I think it goes back for leagues into the mountain, but I can't say for sure. I sensed someone there, a presence of evil that took my breath away. Still, I went into the cave, and there I found body after body, laid out on shelves of rock and covered with cloth. I thought at first that it was just that, the bodies of our children. But then I saw the cloths move so slowly and slightly with each breath that the children took. Such small breaths, but they are such small children. I believe they live, just in a deep sleep from which they do not wake."

Shaen put one hand to her mouth and the other on her heart. "They live? Our children live?" She cried out and turned to Aelf with tears streaming down her face. Aelf stood abruptly and walked a few steps away from the group. His head was bowed, and his shoulders shook, but not a sound escaped his lips. They all sat completely still and silent, looking at each other or at the ground. At last, Aelf turned and sat down with them. Taking Shaen's hand, he questioned Granny, "I want to believe you, Matilda. The fates know that I want to believe you. But how? How did the children come to be in that cave? And why have we not found it? We have searched these mountains for months with the best trackers the Folk have. Who would have taken these children, and why? For the love of the fates, why? Why would anyone want to take our children?"

"I don't know that yet. I have not discovered that, but I told Erik Tamen about this, and he was on his way to find out more and to try to bring our children home. Yet, I believe this is not a task for a single man alone. I think there is an evil that lives within that cave that would make it impossible for one man alone to bring the children home. And yet, in my heart, I believe it can be done. I am not sure how, but I believe this. I ask this of you and the Folk. Let me stay here while Erik heals. Let me work with Ronan and perhaps you, Shaen, and any others who might have the gift of telling and traveling. Let us work together for our common cause. What do you say, Aelf? Will you work with us? Will you allow us to work with you?"

18

ANOTHER CHANGE

Sean and Doireann marched through the village to the center of the square. Years before, the village had begun with just a few cottages built around a square with a good empty space in the middle. Over the years, a cooperage, a small inn and tavern, and a church joined the few homes around the square. The inn, with its rock foundation, was the sturdiest building in the village. The church was small, painted white as it should be, and thatched with the best straw the villagers could give. The cooper expanded to include a small forge for working metal into tools and shoeing an occasional horse should a traveler come through who needed it. Gradually, green grass grew in the square, and now, the villagers took turns bringing their sheep in to graze the grass short in the summer. The women of the village took turns planting flowers around the square, giving the boys the job of keeping them safe from the grazing sheep.

The men had built a long, low building at the far end of the square, in which they held their council and village meetings, but everyone agreed that during the spring and summer, the square was the best place to hold meetings. It became their habit to bring a basket lunch and maybe a small bottle of ale, spread a blanket on the grass, and listen to the council.

The square became the place to hold Beltane in the spring or harvest festival in the fall. Long trestle tables and benches were hauled out and covered with bright-colored cloths. The women would outdo themselves roasting meats and vegetables, baking pies and fresh bread. Everyone joined in the celebrations, feasting until the sun went down, at which time someone brought out a fiddle, and music would fill the night air. Children would chase each other around the square, while young men and women danced and older men and women enjoyed their ease with pipe or gossip.

At some point, it was decided that a bell tower would be just the thing to call the villagers to a meeting or a celebration. The men of the village pooled their resources of good timber planed into boards, and everyone gathered to watch the tower take shape and form. The council sent off for an iron bell, and though it took months before it arrived on the back of a tinker's wagon, they all agreed that it was worth the wait. It took two stout men to climb the tower and haul the bell up by a rope, while a third man swung it into line and hung it. They attached a long rope that hovered about six feet above the ground. Any closer, and naughty boys were wont to try to ring the bell. Still, even at that height, they were known to stand on one another's shoulders, grab the rope, and give it a good yank before scurrying off to hide and laugh. Many a young boy had felt the sting of a switch after being caught ringing the bell. After a few such whippings, the joke lost its appeal, and the bell was used once more for its original purpose.

Now Sean snatched up the rope from the bell tower and gave it a mighty tug, then three more short, fast ones. That was the "all call" signal to the villagers. It meant that there was village business that was urgent, and everyone was to meet in the square. Sean stepped down from the tower and waited for the villagers to assemble. Some came at a run, others more leisurely, as if they knew there was something afoot that they didn't want to hear.

When at last there was a good number of people, Sean stood on the steps leading to the tower and cleared his throat. "Gather round!" He tried to make the command with authority, but it came out somewhere between a sheep's bleat and a frog's croak. He cleared his throat and glared at the villagers all milling around and whispering among themselves.

"Where's Erik?" they muttered. "Where's our mayor?"

"He's the one who should be calling this meeting."

Sean tried again, with more success. "Listen up!" he cried out. All heads turned in his direction, most with frowns on their faces, but some with even a glint of laughter.

"Where's Erik?" This time there was no secret who put forth that question. Tilly's father, Quinn, stepped forward. "Where is he? Why are you ringing the bell? You've no right to do that, Sean."

Doireann stepped forward and stood next to Sean. "By the light, he does have the right and the authority. Erik Tamen gave him the job of mayor and constable, and I heard it all. I witnessed it to be true. Sean is your mayor now, and you best be giving him the respect he's due!"

This announcement brought a series of guffaws and chuckles, as well as a few outraged voices. Again, it was Quinn who spoke for the villagers. "All right. Let's all calm down now and hear him out. Sean, what is this that Doireann is saying? Where's Erik? You owe us a good explanation, I think."

Sean drew himself up to his full height, squared his shoulders, and cleared his throat again. "Yes, I do owe you an explanation, and if you will listen, I am happy to give it to you. After months and months of anxiety and fear while our children were snatched right from under our noses, Erik Tamen finally decided that it was time he took some action. It was finally time he acted as our mayor and constable. He left this morning to travel to the mountains. For some reason, he thinks the children are there, and he has gone to find them. It took months for him to take our problems seriously and months for him to work up the courage to go, but go he has. And as he was leaving town, he came and found Doireann and me to tell us. He insisted that the village needed someone to stand in for him while he was gone, and he insisted that I was the best man for the job. I wasn't sure about it, but he seemed very determined that I was the best choice. I promised him that I would do my best for you and keep everything running smoothly till when and if he returns. Now, there need to be some changes made while he is gone, and we might as well start now with those changes."

Quinn looked doubtful. "You say Erik came and found you before he left and insisted that you take over for him? I was just with him this morning, and he said no such thing to me. And what do you mean, 'if he returns'?"

"Of course not, Quinn. He knew you were grieving for Tilly. He's not going to bother you with trivial details when he knows you are in a state of worry. Like Doireann says, she heard it all. We were just out for a morning stroll when he came rushing up to us. We were of a mind to greet him and keep walking, but no, he insisted that we stop and listen to him. He apologized for taking so long to look for the children and begged me to take the job while he was gone. And yes, Quinn, I am certain he will return. Those were his words, not mine. Trust me!"

Quinn looked doubtful, but how could he argue with Sean? He turned and faced the villagers, who for the most part shrugged their shoulders. Too defeated from the months of worry and fear, they muttered among themselves.

"What harm can there be? It's only for a few days, true? When Erik returns with the children, everything will be as it was before."

Quinn listened to their voices and turned back to Sean. "We agree that you will be the mayor and constable, but just for the few days that it takes Erik to bring our children home."

Sean's look was one of satisfaction. "All right, then. I have some directions for you. First of all, no one is to be out alone. You must be in twos or more to go anywhere. And I mean anywhere—your neighbor's house, your gardens, anywhere. No children are allowed outside without at least two adults to watch over them. No one is to take knitting or basket repair when they are watching children. You watch children and nothing else. Nothing should distract you from the business of keeping children safe. And lastly, anyone with children must all sleep together in the common meeting room. You can take blankets and make pallets on the floor, but all children must sleep together from now on. Lastly, we take turns guarding the doors and windows to the meeting room as long as there are children present.

"There will be a rotation of men working the fields. I want at least six men working together for safety. I will post the work crews and the fields they are to work. I want the women in the village to work in crews cleaning and cooking. I will post the crews and the schedule for that as well. If we all stay together all the time, we can stay safe from whatever it is that's troubling our village."

The villagers looked at each other in puzzlement. Work the fields together? Clean and cook together? Sleep together? They shook their heads but quietly filed back to their cottages. Too tired to argue, too discouraged to fight, they would stay quiet and wait for the voice of reason to return in Erik Tamen.

When the villagers had all drifted away, Sean turned to Doireann, expecting approval, maybe even praise for his performance. Her face was the same dour one that greeted him every morning and complained at him every day, all day. "What do you think, my dearest? Do I make a good mayor, do you think?"

"Hmmph. I didn't like the way you let that Quinn talk to you. He should show more respect. You should demand respect from them. We'll see how long this lasts, unless you get more of a backbone." With that, she turned on her heel and walked away, leaving Sean to drag himself after her.

The days that followed were filled with confusion as Sean posted lists of work crews and fields, starting with his own fields. He made sure that a crew of women showed up at his cottage to clean and cook for Doireann. After all, there should be some reward for taking the job of mayor, right? He spent his days supervising the work details, while he sent Doireann to make sure the villagers were watching over children according to his directions. At night, he posted guards around the meeting room after the children were safely locked in. Claiming to need his sleep to maintain order in the village, he tottered off for a good night's sleep himself.

Increasingly, the villagers grew more and more disgruntled with the turn of events. Erik Tamen never made the other villagers tend his fields or clean his house. More likely, he and Guin would be helping others take care of their business if they were unable.

"Remember the time he helped you get your wheat in when you broke your leg and couldn't work?" they asked. *"Remember when Guin fixed enough stew to feed us for three days when we were sick and didn't have the strength to cook for ourselves? Remember when they both fed our sheep and pulled the weeds from the garden when we were taking care of our da? Now we work for Sean and Doireann? How did this happen?"*

The villagers met in small groups and complained to one another. And yet, they were tired of fighting and worried that they would never see their children again. *"It's just for a few days,"* they kept telling themselves. But the days dragged on and on, and finally a small group went to see Quinn.

He listened patiently to their complaints and asked them what they thought he could do about the situation. One of the villagers spoke up, "We don't know, Quinn, but my fields are falling into ruin because we're busy working in Sean's. Not only do our wives cook, but they take the meat and vegetables to do it, so Sean and Doireann are eating like royalty, and our wives are too tired to cook anything decent for us. Not a one of us has had a good night's sleep, between standing guard or sleeping on pallets on the meetinghouse floor. We want to work in our own fields, clean our own houses, and watch over our children ourselves. There hasn't been a child gone missing since Tilly." Quinn met that last statement with a glare that would set a woodpile on fire. "I'm sorry, Quinn. I didn't mean anything by it. I just want to work my fields, sit in my clean house, and have a good warm meal that my wife has fixed me."

Quinn sighed. "I understand. I really do. Let me talk with Sean and see if I can reason with him."

Quinn found Sean in the square, nailing a new list of crew members and assignments by the bell tower. Scanning it quickly, he saw that once again men were assigned to Sean's fields and women were cooking and cleaning for Doireann. "Sean, the villagers have come to me with a problem that I hope you can help us with."

"Well, Quinn, I am your mayor. It's my job to solve problems for the villagers, so I am happy to listen and do whatever I can to help." This was said offhandedly as he nailed the list of women assigned to clean his wife's house and cook her meals.

"It's like this, Sean. We appreciate that you want to keep everyone safe, especially the children. But the truth is, we seem to be working for you and Doireann and no one else. The men need to get to their own fields, and the women need to keep their own houses and cook their own meals. I think you either need to let everyone go back to their own work or divide up the work a little more evenly, so it isn't just you who prospers from it."

Sean gave Quinn his full attention. "What are you talking about? The village has never been safer, the remaining children are all still with us, and work is getting done. I volunteered my fields, and Doireann was kind enough to let the women work in her house, until everyone got used to doing it this way. As soon as the schedules work smoothly, I'll start sending the men out to other fields and houses. You can't possibly think that I hope to use this to enrich myself. Quinn, you know I care about the villagers more than I care about myself. I've done the best job of being mayor that anyone has ever done. The crews are organized, the work is getting done, and everyone is safe.

"Now, you can't say that happened when Erik Tamen was mayor. No sir, you can't say that. In fact, what you could say was that Erik was a disorganized man who only went around making jokes and telling stories. He was completely unprepared to handle any kind of threat to our community. I, on the other hand, am in complete control of the situation. Everything is running smoothly, everyone is safe, the fields have never looked better, and the meals the women are cooking are the best they've ever been. No, my friend, you're wrong. I am the best mayor this village has ever seen. Now, you just take a look at this list. I think you're due in my fields first thing tomorrow morning, and your good wife will be helping Doireann in the house." With that, he picked up his nails and hammer and set off toward his home, leaving Quinn stammering behind.

Quinn took a while to think things through. Never one to make a quick decision, he decided to sleep on the problem until morning, but in the morning, when it was his turn to work in Sean's fields, he decided that he had had enough. "I'm not even sure I buy his story about Erik asking him to be mayor. It seems like Erik would have said something to me if he planned on doing that, if for no other reason than I would have talked him out of the half-witted idea!"

As soon as he finished his morning meal, he strode through the village to the square. He looked long and hard at the lists that Sean had posted the day before and, after reading them, ripped them off the posts. He reached for the bell rope and pulled it, one long pull followed by three short ones. He sat down on the steps and waited for what he knew was coming. It didn't take long to prove himself right.

Looking down the road, he saw Sean and Doireann coming at a run, Sean in front, with Doireann's plump legs working to catch up to him. Quinn waited patiently and calmly. He wasn't sure exactly what he planned on saying, but he figured the other villagers were mad enough that they just might speak up. At any rate, he knew one thing for sure. He wasn't going to Sean's fields this morning, or any other morning, and if he thought for one minute that he was going to do without a hot meal at the end of his day so that his wife could fix food for Doireann, then their thinking was all wrong. He sat back, folded his arms, and waited for the storm to hit. He was not disappointed.

"What is the meaning of this? You can't call a general meeting. You have no authority, Quinn. You people, go back to what you were doing. Go on, there's no meeting taking place. Quinn made a mistake calling it. Go on about your business. And you, Quinn, you should be in my field right now. Get your tools and get moving!" Sean's face was red, and spittle flew as he waved his arms and yelled.

"No sir, I won't. I think the whole village needs to hear what I have to say, Sean. We'll wait until everyone is here, and then I'll say what I have to say. Do you think we need to ring the bell again? Maybe someone didn't hear it?"

Sean cursed under his breath and started to stomp away, but by then the villagers were gathering, and to walk away would look like weakness. This was something Sean couldn't abide. Doireann pushed her way to the front, shoving men and women aside with her bulk. She grabbed Sean's arm and pinched it until he blanched and sucked in his breath.

"Do something!" she hissed at him. "We're about to lose the best thing we've ever had because of your spineless attitude. Now do something right now!"

The villagers milled around, whispering to each other and watching Quinn sitting quietly on the steps and Sean and Doireann working to recover their wits.

Finally, Quinn stood up and addressed the people. "You've come to me, some of you, with complaints about the way Sean is running things here. You've told me your fields are being neglected, and your homes are not running themselves while your wives take care of Doireann's home. You've told me you're tired of sleeping on the meetinghouse floor or standing guard all night. You've told me you want to tend your own fields and homes and watch over your children yourselves. Now, I took your complaints to Sean, and he told me that the village has never been run better than it is now and that he is the best mayor we've ever had the privilege of having. Now, I disagree, but I thought he should hear it from you all, not just from me."

The words were no sooner out of Quinn's mouth than the people all began speaking at once, filling the air with their complaints and grievances. Sean looked from one to the other, dumbfounded. What betrayal! What a pack of traitors! What he did he did for their own good, them and the children. Hadn't the children been safer since he took over? What more could they ask? Why, his plans were just now working smoothly. What an ungrateful group of people!

Sean raised his hand to quiet the people. "What do you think you're doing? You know Erik begged me to take over for him while he is away. You know that everything I do, I do for the good of the village. You never questioned him; why are you pestering me with your complaints?"

This was met with another round of yelling from the people.

They all seemed to raise their voices at once, hoping to get a point across.

Quinn stepped forward and held up his hand for quiet. Immediately, the people were silent and waited for him to speak. "It's like this, Sean. If you really want to make a difference, I've thought of a way for you to do just that. I've been thinking on this all night, and here's what I've come up with. Erik Tamen is out there in those mountains somewhere all by himself. Now, I know you want to help, and here's how you can make a difference. We don't care about fields or homes or even meals. We care about children, our children. I think the best way for you to help is to give us your lists and schedules and let us run the village for you. You take off and go find Erik Tamen and be of good help to him. All this time, you've been mumbling in the background about Erik doing something. Well, maybe what's good for him is good for you. You want to make yourself important, then go help him find our children and bring them home." Quinn stepped back and folded his arms and watched the crowd and Sean.

Sean immediately began to stammer and stutter denials and excuses, but his voice was drowned out by voices from the people. *"That's the best idea I've heard in days, Sean. You go help him find our children. Make yourself useful to us all. We'll take care of the village ourselves."* They all turned to one another and nodded their agreement. As one body, they turned to Sean and looked him dead in the eye.

Doireann grabbed him and dragged him off around the bell tower. "Now look what you've done. Well, I see no choice to it. You leave the lists and jobs to be done, and you go after Erik. I've gotten used to having my house cleaned and my meals cooked, and I don't plan on giving that up anytime soon. If they're willing to keep up the work while you go, then I say go!"

"But, dearest, I don't know the first thing about those mountains. How would I ever find Erik? What if I get lost? What if I never come back to you?"

"I guess you'll be marked a hero, something you cannot ever hope to achieve while you're alive. You go, I say, or I will make your life so miserable you'll wish you'd gone ten times over." She pushed him back to face the crowd.

Sean wiped his hands on his pants and swallowed once or twice. "If you think that's the best way for me to help you, then I will do it. I trust you will keep looking after Doireann while I'm gone."

The villagers all shook their heads in agreement. Quinn clapped Sean on the back, causing him to take one or two steps forward under the force of it. "You rest assured, we'll look after everything while you're gone. I say you get ready and leave first thing tomorrow morning, Sean. No telling how far Erik has gotten by now. We'll find someone willing to cook and clean for Doireann, I'm sure. It's just a matter of looking in the right place for the right person."

19

TIME TO LEAVE

The next morning found Sean rummaging around his bare cottage cupboards looking for food to pack, a bottle for water, and maybe, just maybe, his long-lost tobacco pouch. "This is really unfair, Doireann. I was just getting our fields in good order. Why, next I was going to have the men start working on this cottage. I fancied a better front porch, maybe a new chimney if rock could be found, and I'm sure I could get the women to sew some pretty curtains for the windows. We were going to be better off than we've ever been. Now what will happen?"

Doireann frowned at him from her chair in front of the fire. Waving away the smoke that drifted into her face, she squinted at him across the room. "I knew it was too good to be true. I knew you couldn't make them keep it up. You just don't have the backbone for it, Sean. I'll be lucky if Quinn finds anyone to keep this house and cook for me. That's the most important thing right now."

Sean hung his head but did not argue with Doireann. He stuffed meat and cheese into his pack, added a few wizened potatoes, and though he placed his pipe in carefully, he found not so much as one flake of tobacco to pack. Sighing, he lifted the pack and took up his walking stick from the corner. "Will you wish me farewell and good luck, wife?"

Doireann waved a hand from her place by the fire, and Sean went quietly out the door.

He stood and gazed at the far-off mountains for several minutes, wishing he knew any way on this green earth to get out of the mess he found himself in at the moment. Caught between the villagers and Doireann, he had no choice but to head out. Maybe he could be gone overnight and come back and tell them he found no sign of Erik Tamen. No, they would just send him out alone to find the children. Maybe he could ask Quinn to come with him. No, Quinn would never agree to that. They had never been friends, not like Quinn and Erik.

In fact, standing on his porch at that moment, he could not think of one person in the village that he could ask for help. His shoulders slumped, and he felt tears gather in his eyes. He wanted nothing more in this world than to sit by his fire, smoke his pipe, and watch his wife darn his socks or stitch curtains for their cottage. Instead, he would be wandering the mountains looking for a man who had no use for him and children who teased him and made his life miserable. Clutching his walking stick in his hand, he flung the pack over his shoulders and stepped down from the porch.

It was past midday when Sean stopped for his meal. Pulling his meager bit of food from his pack, he sat down to face the mountains with his back against a tree. It felt good to sit after the miles of walking across the valley, but in truth, he was almost proud of himself for the distance he had put between himself and the village. Maybe this was possible. Maybe he could find Erik Tamen and help him rescue the children.

He took time to enjoy the dream of arriving back in the village at the head of a stream of children, with Erik bringing up the rear, of course. The villagers would run out to greet him, clap him on his back, and congratulate him before turning to find their children. Oh, the square would be full of feasting and merriment, and he would sit at the table of honor. All night, people would come up to thank him and ask what they could do to repay him. He would tell them it was his job as temporary mayor, and he was proud to do it.

Sean leaned his head back against the tree, thinking these pleasant thoughts. Shortly, his head begin to nod toward his chest and his eyes closed. A faint snore issued from his mouth as sleep overtook him.

The evening shadows were long by the time Sean woke up with a start. What on this good green earth was he doing sleeping the day away? He needed to be on his way to find Erik. As it was, he would have to find a place to sleep tonight. Looking around, he saw that there was a deep cut in the hills before they rose to the mountains. It looked as if a valley would be up that cut, and perhaps a stream for water would run through it. He gathered his belongings and hurried toward the cut.

Once there, he found some rocks he could shelter behind, with a rock wall at his back. He felt safe with the wall behind him and the rocks in front. The only problem was that the rocks gave him no comfort for sleeping. He looked around for grass to pull to make himself a bed, but grass was thin and sparse, not nearly long enough to comfort his poor bones. He found an elm tree and stripped some of the young branches off to carry back behind the rocks. Piling them up, he thought they looked very meager, but it was the best he could do. Wrapping himself in his cloak, he lay down to sleep.

The night was full of noises, noises that seemed to be right above him or just off to the side. He wished he had a fire, but he hadn't thought to bring flint with him, so there would be no comfort from one tonight. Lying on his bed of elm branches, he realized once more how unprepared he was for this task. The daydreams of rescuing the children and leading them all home to the village seemed silly to him now. He was ashamed that instead of walking, he had spent the afternoon in thoughts that would never happen. More than likely, he would wander around the hills, never even making it up to the mountains, until he finally went back home in disgrace.

He couldn't bear the thought of going back to the village without Erik or the children. It would be the same thing all over again. *Sean the do-nothing. Sean the lazy. Sean the laughingstock.* Was it too much to ask that he be given a little respect? These were the thoughts that swirled around in this head as he finally closed his eyes to sleep on the first night in the hills.

Morning found him stiff and sore from a night on rocks and branches. He hobbled to a likely spot to find water and was rewarded with enough to splash on his face and fill his bottle. He opened his pack to realize that he had eaten almost all his food yesterday. He had a small bit of moldy cheese and a handful of potatoes that had been roasted days before. They looked like little old man faces, all wrinkled and pinched. Nevertheless, he ate the last of the cheese and chewed the potatoes one at a time to make them last.

Swallowing the last of the potatoes, he realized he had a choice to make. Go home a disgrace or go forward. Going forward was an uncertain course. How would he find food? How would he find Erik? And yet, the unknown was easier to think about then the known disgrace that awaited him in the village. With a sigh, he gathered up his pack and his walking stick and turned his face toward the mountains.

For the first time, Sean looked at the highest peak and saw the black swirl of clouds at the top. They looked as if they were moving, ever moving, but did not blow away.

He stopped and stared. *I never noticed that before. Have those clouds always been there, blowing around and around like that?* The longer he stared, the more he became convinced that the clouds had something to do with the children and Erik. He leaned on his walking stick and puzzled it out. *Could it be that there is something here that we don't understand? Could it be that Erik knew something he didn't tell us? I'm not sure, but I think I'll keep an eye on those clouds and see what happens. If they are still there, looking the same, it might mean something. At any rate, it gives me something to set my course by.*

Determined to waste no more time, he kept his eyes on the clouds at the top of the mountain and started walking. The way soon became rockier, and the path he found wound around the hills, back and forth instead of straight up. He paused to drink water and check on the clouds, which remained the same as he had seen in the morning. The path led him through small canyons and upward toward the mountains. With no food left in his pack, he found himself dreaming of roasts of beef and stuffed chicken with potatoes and gravy. His stomach rumbled and he felt weak in his knees, but for once determination overruled his instincts to hunker down and let someone else do the hard work.

He pressed on over rocks and through small streams, where he refreshed himself with the cool water. He found some berries that the birds had neglected to find, and snatching up handfuls, he gobbled them down and drank more of his water. Nightfall found him well into the base of the mountains. From this angle, he could no longer look up and see the clouds. Finding a cave with a small waterfall trickling down beside it, he thought it made no better place for him to spend the second night. If only the villagers could see him now— hungry, tired, and just a little scared, but still here after all. That had to count for something!

20

SEAN ON HIS OWN

The next morning dawned dark and cloudy, with a stiff breeze blowing from the north. Sean shivered when he came out of his cave. Wrapping his cloak around him, he wished for something for his morning meal. Anything at this point would be welcome. He sat on some rocks and watched the trees around him. *How do you find food in these mountains?* he wondered to himself. He idly watched a bird fly into the tree across from him. The bird landed in a nest and, folding her wings, settled down. *Wait! A bird in a nest—perhaps eggs?* He scrambled up from his seat and walked over to the tree. Looking up, he realized the nest was a bit higher than it looked from the rock he'd sat on, but he had loved climbing trees as a boy. Perhaps he hadn't lost all his skills.

Grabbing the lowest branch, Sean pulled himself up until his feet were braced against the tree trunk. From that point, it was easy to use one hand to grab the next branch and pull his feet up to the first one, where he could stand quite comfortably. After that, it was much like climbing a ladder, one branch at a time, until he could peer over the edge of the nest. Four eggs he counted. Not the biggest eggs he'd ever seen, but they would do. He started to grab all four and then stopped himself. What would the bird think when she came back to the nest and her eggs were all gone?

He reached carefully into the nest and, without touching the last egg, pulled three out of the nest. He placed them tenderly into his pocket and climbed back down to solid ground.

Once on the ground, he looked at the eggs. Pale blue in color, with darker spots on them, they were about the size of a plum. *Not bad,* he thought, *but how will I cook them?* He sat down on his rock with the eggs in his hands, pondering the problem. With no flint, making a fire was going to be difficult, but he guessed he could try. He knew that certain rocks, when hit together, might create a spark. After all, when he had forgotten to bank up the coals in the fireplace before going to bed, he was forced to start a new fire in the morning. He searched around and found rocks of all shapes and sizes, but despite banging them together until his hands hurt, he never saw a single spark fly.

Putting the rocks aside, he looked at the eggs once more. He could feel his stomach rumbling from the emptiness within. When was the last time he had eaten? Days ago? Well, maybe yesterday at midday. Still, that was a long time to go with no food. He sighed, knowing what he had to do but not sure if he could do it. He took one of the eggs and gently cracked it on the rock. Opening it carefully so that the egg was held in one half of the shell, like his mother used to do when she made cakes, he raised the egg to his mouth and tilted his head back. The egg slid down his throat as if down a greased pipe. It hit his stomach with a lurch, but immediately he felt better for something in it. Without stopping to think about it, he cracked the other two eggs and, tipping his head back, slid them down his throat.

He washed his face and hands in the small trickle of water next to the cave, drank his fill from water cupped in his hands, and filled his water bottle to the top. Placing the cork in it to keep the water from spilling, he packed it in his pack and picked up his walking stick. He would keep a sharp eye out for more birds, and certainly some more of those berries that he found yesterday. It wouldn't hurt to keep an eye out for rocks that could be used to start a fire. Too bad he didn't really know what kind would be best, but if he looked hard enough, he might get lucky. Sean picked up his walking stick and flung his mostly empty pack over his shoulder. With one last look at the tree with the nest, he started up the trail to see just what the day would bring for him.

Oddly, out here in the middle of the mountains, with no idea where he was going or how he was going to get there, he felt freer than he had felt in years. Out here there was no nagging voice telling him he wasn't good enough, that he would never amount to anything. No ramshackle cottage falling down around his ears to remind him of the house he once lived in and would never live in again. No villagers to ignore him and push him aside. There was just him and the mountains. He had to rely on himself, no one else. By the fates, he would do it.

By midday, he was once again feeling the pangs of hunger. The three raw eggs that he'd swallowed that morning were long gone. *Well, they would be,* he thought, *as hard as I've been walking and climbing. I'm going to need more than that if I'm to do this job.*

He began peering up into the trees, looking for more birds' nests, but none were readily available. Berries seemed to have disappeared the higher he climbed. He found a small stream trickling down the rocks and sat beside it, pondering the problem of food. With no bow or arrow, small game was out of the question. He wasn't much of a hunter anyway. In fact, he wasn't sure if he could actually kill a living creature. And then there was the problem of a fire. He might be able to eat raw eggs, but he sure enough was opposed to eating raw meat.

Fish! That's it, he thought. *Where there is water, there are fish.* He walked up and down the length of the stream as far as he could before running into rocks too big to clamber over. Not a fish did he find. Not a single thing to eat in the stream. Walking back to where he started, he sat and thought some more.

Idly, he picked up some rocks and threw them against the bigger rocks around him. He threw harder and harder the more frustrated he became at the lack of food. Suddenly, the tall, dry grass around the rocks began to smoke. Astonished, he walked over and leaned down to see what could have caused the smoke. The small smoke became a bigger plume, though still not very big. Before his eyes, a small flame licked out of the grass. Without thinking, he grabbed a small handful of dry grass and threw it into the flame, and it grew.

"I'll be! I started a fire!" Looking around for the source of the fire, he found the rocks he had been throwing. Scooting them out with his foot to cool, he looked more closely at them. Sure enough, one of them looked a lot like the piece of flint he kept on his fireplace mantel at home to light his fire with in the event the coals went cold. He bent to pick it up but quickly snatched his hand back from the hot rock. Laughing at himself, he moved the rock again with his foot, farther away from the burning grass. He fed the fire some small sticks and soon enough had a good fire going. He picked up some of the bigger rocks nearby and stacked them around the fire to keep it inside the boundary. *No sense burning the forest down,* he thought.

Sean sat by his fire and thought harder than he'd ever thought before. He had fire now and could have fire whenever he wanted it, so the problem of eating raw food was less than before. The problem still was no food available.

He searched again and found some wild onions growing by the stream. A little farther down, there were some wild rice plants that the birds hadn't eaten. Gathering the onions and the grains of rice, he carried them all back in the folds of his shirt gathered up to hold them. He found a good, flat rock and laid it near the fire until it grew hot. He cleaned the onions and washed them in the stream. He stripped the rice off the plants and laid them on the flat rock with the onions. They popped and sizzled after a while, and the onions smelled delicious as they cooked. He scooped it all up in his hands and ate it, a little at a time. He wished for a nice piece of lamb to lay on the rock and cook, but there was no such thing for him.

It was not the best-tasting dish he'd ever had, but it filled his belly. Then again, Doireann wasn't much of a cook—maybe it was the best meal he'd eaten in a long time. No one to glare at him or nag him while he ate. Birds flew overhead or sang in the tree branches. He listened to the sound of the stream tripping over the rocks and marveled at the sight of clouds chasing each other across the sky. When was the last time he had taken a moment to appreciate these things? When was the last time he had even noticed them? He smiled to himself and remembered a young boy, many years ago, who had settled down in a field of hay and watched the clouds drift through the sky. That was so many years ago, and he was a far different person now. Maybe this time alone in the mountains would be an opportunity to find that young boy again.

He had a way to make fire and a small bit of food in him. Now, if he just had a pinch of tobacco for his pipe. He took the pipe out of his pack and smelled the bowl deeply. Oh, it did smell good. *There's nothing like a good pipe after a meal*, he thought.

Sean decided that he might as well stay near his fire for the rest of the day and night. First thing in the morning, he'd set out again looking for Erik Tamen. In the meantime, he had a nice, cozy place to rest. He wrapped his cloak around him and sat with his back against the rocks. Stretching out his legs, he wished the villagers could see him now. Feeding himself, making a fire, braving the mountains. There was more to him than they knew, he thought. He settled himself back and closed his eyes.

When he woke, his fire had gone out, and it was the darkest night he'd ever seen. No moon above, though the night sky glittered and shone with a thousand lights from stars thrown across it like seeds across a field. He felt the coals and found they were still warm. *I should have gathered more wood before I fell asleep*, he thought.

He stood up and walked hesitantly forward, scraping his feet as he went to avoid tripping over something unseen. He heard the cracking of small sticks under his feet. Bending down, he gathered up as many as he could find in the dark and carried them back to his coals. Stirring the coals up until they glowed, he fed the sticks in, a few at a time, to keep from smothering the small flames. In no time, he had a good fire again.

In the distance, the eerie sound of a wolf howling raised the hairs on the back of his neck. *Wolves! I never thought of wolves. Of course there are wolves here in the mountains! What was I thinking?*

By the glow of his small fire, he gathered up more wood. Determined to stay awake and feed the fire, he leaned against the rock but kept his eyes open and on the flames. He wished for a friend to keep watch, but he must learn to rely on himself. He could do this; he knew he could!

The second morning found him stiff and cold in the early dawn light. His fire was smoking and leaped into flames when he stirred it and added some wood. Still, he couldn't just stay here by his fire. With no food, he would soon starve. And how was he to find Erik Tamen if he just sat here?

He ate the last of the wild onions and rice, made sure the fire was completely out, and filled his bottle from the stream. Checking to see that his piece of flint rock was safely in his pack, he headed up the path for another day of adventure.

21

THE CAVE

Granny stopped outside Ronan's dwelling and called out a morning greeting.

"Come in, Matilda, come in." Ronan swept aside the beautiful wool blanket she used as her summer door and gestured for Granny to enter.

"You will see our patient is much improved this morning, Matilda. He is sleeping now, but he woke early this morning and asked for food. I fixed him some broth, and he laughed! Matilda, the man laughed! He said, 'Do I look like I could live on broth, woman? I need something a bit stronger than broth if I am to get out of this bed.'

"Can you believe that? I fixed him some cakes, meat, and cheese, and he ate every bite. His eyes were falling shut before he finished chewing the last bite, but he smiled and thanked me for the food. He said he hadn't eaten in two days, he reckoned. Two days, Matilda? The man has been here a fortnight with us!"

Granny bent down to look closely at Erik as he lay sleeping. His breathing was deep and even, and a small snore escaped from his lips now and again. Granny felt his head. No fever!

"Praise the fates, Ronan. You did it! You healed him! Your skills as a healer are improving, and you are learning the arts. I am so pleased, Ronan, indeed I am!"

Granny accepted the proffered cup of tea that Ronan held out for her, and they went outside to sit in the morning sun. There was a chill in the air that had not been there when Granny and Conor arrived. *Snow would be flying soon*, she thought. *If we don't get the children out before then, we won't get them out at all.*

"Ronan, please feed Erik as much as you can stuff down the man. It most likely won't be a problem. As I recall, he's a healthy eater." She chuckled as she said this and cast her eyes up to the sky. Sure enough, dark clouds were drifting across the valleys between the mountains. *Snow clouds if I ever saw them*, she thought. *We might get a little snow, but maybe not so much, and maybe if we are lucky, it will melt before we leave here.* She sat and drank her tea with Ronan in comfortable silence.

The women had become close in the days since Granny arrived in the Mountain Folk village. While she worked with other women as well, it was Ronan who by far had the greatest gift of sight and travel. Already, Granny had taught her to travel around the mountains nearby. Soon she expected to teach her how to go to the valleys below them and see how the lowlanders lived. She could teach Ronan so much, but sometimes it was better to see for yourself. If Ronan could watch a good healer mix her herbs and brew teas and make poultices that could take pain away and heal everything from skin ulcers to rashes, she would learn so much more than what she could learn from Granny just telling her. While she had many of her herbs with her, the cupboards in her cottage held a treasure trove of medicines. If only she could have brought more with her.

"Ronan, when do you think Erik will be strong enough to travel?"

Ronan started at the question. "I think you would be better able to answer your own question, Matilda. You are the healer that I hope to be one day, but I am far from it now."

"No, you are his healer. Not me. It must be you who says when he will be able to travel. Part of the responsibility of a healer is to make these difficult decisions and give the best advice you are able to give.

Being a healer is more than mixing teas, my dear. You have to be able to evaluate a person's strength and resilience. Everyone heals at a different rate, and the sooner you recognize that, the better off you'll be. And so will the people you look after. They will look to you to give them that advice, and you do them no good service if you duck away from that part of your duties."

Ronan blushed at the admonition from Granny. "You are right. It is my job, but I still need your advice to give my advice. I think if he keeps eating the way he ate this morning, he should begin to regain his strength in a day or two. I think the test will be when he stands. Has the head injury affected his balance? Will he be able to walk? Will he even be able to sit up?"

"I think I can do both." A gruff voice from the doorway startled both women. Turning as one, they gaped at Erik Tamen, who stood with one hand on the rock wall to steady himself, but still, was standing. He swayed just a little, but only if you looked closely at him would you notice it. "If it's not too much to ask, could I join you for a cup of tea in the sunshine? By the looks of it, it's a fair day, and I believe I have been in that dark cave for far too long."

Ronan jumped up before Granny managed to get her feet under her. She grabbed one of Erik's arms and slid her shoulder under it to give him support. Walking in step, she guided him to the bench and carefully sat him down, pushing him against the rock wall to rest.

Erik grinned at her. "You were right. That took about all I had in me to get that far. It was lucky I didn't have to crawl out to you two. That would have made a pretty impression."

Ronan smiled at him but shook her finger in his face. "I am the healer here, and you will listen to me, or I will give you something in your tea that will slow you down. Now sit here and rest while I get your tea."

Erik leaned against the wall and stretched his legs out to the sun. He wiggled his bare toes and closed his eyes. "How did I get here, Granny? And for that matter, where is 'here' anyway?"

"You've been with the Mountain Folk for almost a fortnight, Erik. I believe you fell down a cliff, most likely because you were too thickheaded to take the time to find another path. The Mountain Folk found you and carried you here to Ronan. I believe they had a council meeting to decide what to do with you. Hit you over the head with a rock or let Ronan do what she could to heal you. You see which one they chose."

"I see. Nice of them not to choose the rock. Mountain Folk, you say? I have heard of them. They once lived down in the valleys, didn't they? How long have they been up here in the mountains?"

"For generations, now. They once lived near our village, but before my grandmother's time, there was a falling out, and they were driven from the valley. Since then, they have learned to live here in the mountains, and I think you could say they live quite well. They shun lowlanders, as they call us, but something has happened here that's caused them to try to trust us."

"And how did you come to be here, Granny? Now that I think of it, all these questions are making my head hurt. Maybe we could talk more after I get some tea into me."

As if she heard, Ronan appeared with tea in her hand. Erik took it gratefully and blew on it to cool it. The steam headed Granny's way, and she lifted her eyebrows in question at Ronan. Ronan smiled and gave her just the slightest wink.

"Drink your tea, and we'll talk when you are done."

Erik sipped the hot tea and relaxed in the sun. Just as the last drop slid down his throat, he gave a mighty yawn. "I'm sorry, Granny. I don't think I can keep my eyes open, or my mouth, for that matter. Can we talk in just a little while?"

"Of course, Erik. Let Ronan help you back to your bed." Granny smiled to herself. *She will do just fine as a healer*, she thought.

When Ronan reappeared a few moments later, Granny smiled at her. "You are a sneaky one, aren't you? I could smell the valerian root in the tea you brewed, even if Erik couldn't."

"You did tell me that part of my job as a healer was to know when my patient was strong enough to be up and about. I don't think he is yet. A day or so more in bed with good food in him will make all the difference, I think."

Granny nodded. "I agree. No sense wearing himself out before he even starts to recover. I think I will go find Aelf and share the good news."

Aelf was outside his dwelling, restringing his bow with fresh gut line. He looked up as Granny approached. "Good news, Aelf! Erik is awake and talking. Ronan fixed him a good morning meal and he's back asleep, but she feels confident that he will be up and around for good in a day or so."

Aelf set aside the bow and the length of line he was using. "That is good news, Matilda. I've been watching the sky, and I don't like the looks of it. If we aren't in for an early snow, I miss my guess. I think we need to get organized and on the trail soon, or we might not be able to climb all the way to the top."

"Aelf, I'd like to travel there before we leave the village. I'd like to ask Ronan to go with me. She's proved to be very adept at traveling, and although she's never gone that far, I think she could if we did it together. I'd like her to see what I've seen and be able to tell you first-hand. Will you give your permission?"

Aelf chuckled, a deep rumble of a laugh. "You must think I have any say-so over that woman, Matilda. I don't know if you can tell this or not, but Ronan makes up her own mind, and there's not a lot I have to say about it, even as her chief. In our world, healers are set apart to be or do anything they want, except, of course, go to the lowlands. No one is allowed that privilege."

Granny smiled at him. "Let's agree to talk about that whenever we get our children back, what do you say?"

Aelf smiled at her, knowing this was a conversation that was doomed to fail. No sense in letting her think the council would ever let Ronan travel to the valley to study healing, no matter who asked.

Granny found Conor and Wolf sitting outside Cormac's dwelling. Cormac was showing Conor how to soak the supple elm wood and bend it just enough to tie the gut line on it for a strong bow. There was a small stack of arrows fitted with tips and feathers to help them fly true and straight. Conor was turning into a gifted carver and maker of tools and weapons. He would be taking good knowledge from the Mountain Folk back home when he went. He looked up and smiled at Granny. "How's Erik Tamen today?" he asked.

"Good news, Conor, he's awake and eating. You'll be able to see him later today. He was up walking around, and Ronan has him back in bed to continue to gain strength, but she's confident that he will be up to traveling in a day or so."

"That is good news, Granny! I can't tell you how hard it is to sit here, knowing that Tilly is so close and I can't do anything about it."

"I know, child. You've been patient long enough, both you and Wolf. Cormac, I'm going to travel there tonight, and I'm going to ask Ronan to accompany me. I want her to see firsthand that the children are there and how they fare. I want her to be able to come back and tell the Mountain Folk herself. I'd be pleased if you would sit with us while we travel. You too, Conor. It helps to have someone we care for to help pull us back."

"Care for, Granny? Of course I will. I'll meet you at Ronan's dwelling after the evening meal."

Granny nodded and patted his hand. She had seen how Cormac looked at Ronan when he thought no one was watching. She felt sure he had feelings for the healer, but what he didn't know was that Ronan looked at him when she thought he wasn't looking. *Aw, youngsters! If only they would talk to one another and clear up all the confusion!*

Conor and Cormac walked the path from the village to Ronan's dwelling. Cormac looked puzzled and kept talking to himself. Conor watched him out of the corner of his eye and laughed to himself. *He's practicing what to say to Ronan,* he thought.

"Conor, what do you think Matilda meant when she said it helped to have someone who cares for them there when they travel?"

"Granny travels all the time with no one around, so I don't think it's me she's concerned about being there. I'm pretty sure it's you, Cormac."

"Why me, I wonder?"

"Because Ronan is new at traveling, and maybe Granny is worried she'll have a hard time finding her way back. If you are there, it gives her something to aim for, I guess."

Cormac nodded but looked unconvinced. Conor just smiled to himself. *Thickheaded*, he thought. *For such a smart man, he sure is thickheaded!*

When they arrived at Ronan's dwelling, they stood outside and spoke a greeting to let them know they were there. Ronan swept aside the wool blanket, and she and Granny joined them. "Conor, if you want to see Erik, go in now. He's had his evening meal, and I don't think he'll keep his eyes open for long."

Conor went in, eager to see Erik Tamen. The big man had his eyes closed, but as soon as Conor spoke, he opened them, and a huge grin split his face in half. "Oh, Conor, my boy! It is so good to see you! I know why you are here. You must ache to get to Tilly, and I am sorry that I have delayed you and Granny from doing that. I am grateful that you were willing to wait here until I am able. I promise, just give me a day or so, and I will be ready to travel."

Conor sat down cross-legged next to Erik's bed. "I am glad you are alive and feeling better. We were all worried, Erik. Yes, it has been hard to wait, but Granny assured me that Tilly is just sleeping. She has no idea where she is or how long she's been away from us. As long as we can leave soon, and the sooner the better. Granny says there might be snow in the mountains, and if there is, I do not think we'll be able to get anyone out. So you rest and eat. I'll see you soon. Granny and Ronan are going to travel to the cave where the children and Tilly are being kept. They need to find out as much as they can to help us when it is time. You rest, now."

He got up from the ground and started to walk out. Erik looked at him with a frown. When had the boy gotten so self-assured? He remembered Conor as a scrawny, shy boy who avoided the villagers and kept to himself, except when he was with Tilly or Wolf. *But here he is, telling me to rest. The boy is growing up before our eyes. I think that must be what happens when you are tried as he has been tried lately. You either grow up, or you crumble. Good for him!* Erik settled back on his pile of furs and closed his eyes.

Outside, Ronan and Granny sat on one bench with a cup of tea in their hands while Conor sat down next to Cormac. Granny was explaining to Cormac how traveling worked. "It is my hope that we can go to the cave and make sure the children are there. I haven't gone there since before they took Tilly, and I want to make sure she is safe there. It might help us to know why they took our children, what their intentions are for them. You will sit and be very quiet. You won't touch us or talk to us, even if we cry out or start. It is very important that we be left alone. We will feel your presence the whole time we are gone, but you must not do anything that interferes with our work. We may find things there that frighten us and cause us to cry out. Be patient and calm and continue to keep us fixed firmly in your minds. That gives us an anchor to return safely to. I have not needed an anchor for years, but Ronan is new to this, and she might need to know that you are here, Cormac. Conor, I want you here for another reason that I will tell you as soon as I can."

Both Cormac and Conor assured them that they would follow Granny's instructions to the letter, no matter how difficult it might be. Ronan and Granny finished sipping their tea and sat back against the rock wall. Closing their eyes, their breathing became slower and deeper, as if they were asleep. Conor and Cormac looked at one another, but their lips remained sealed.

Ronan found herself outside a cave so deep and dark that she could not see anything past the yawning entrance. There was a rock overhang that meant you might have to bend down just a little to enter the cave. It also meant that it was difficult to see inside. Anyone just walking nearby would be pardoned for missing the entrance altogether. She felt the cold air that blew out of the black depths, and she shivered. Drawing her cloak around her, she felt for Granny's hand and gripped it tightly.

Granny walked toward the entrance to the cave, pulling Ronan along behind her. The air felt stagnant and dead, as if it had been trapped in the cave and not allowed to leave for years. Once inside, they stopped to allow their eyes to adjust to the gloom. Ronan could see shapes on rock platforms, one, two . . . No, as her eyes adjusted, she realized it was dozens and dozens of shapes she was seeing. Her breath caught as she tried to count them, but she soon lost count in the darkness.

Granny led her to one side of the cave and put her finger to her lips, a sign that Ronan was not to make a sound. A tall figure came from the back of the cave and glided silently among the shapes. A woman with coal-black hair that fell below her waist, she was dressed in a sweeping black gown that brushed along the cave floor as she walked. Ronan could hear the whisper of the cloth against the floor, and for some reason, the hair on the back of her neck stood tall, and she shivered once more. The woman trailed her fingers against the shapes and began humming softly, stopping now and again to adjust a covering.

The steady rise and fall of the cloth over the shapes was the only thing that told Ronan that there were children on those platforms. She held her breath as the woman came near to where they stood hidden in the shadows, but at the last moment, she turned and walked down the far side of the cave. Ronan let her breath out slowly. The woman in black paused at a platform and, bending close to the shape, pulled the cloth back. Without thinking, Ronan gasped. She knew that face! It was a face that she had seen since it first learned to totter around their village and was old enough to come and visit with her. Aelf and Shaen's youngest boy, Neall, lay motionless before her. She started forward instinctively, but Granny gripped her arm with an iron hand, and she retreated, shaking with grief.

The woman bent down and whispered something in Neall's ear, and his eyes opened. She touched his arm and murmured again, and he sat up and swung his legs over the side of the platform. Leaving him there, she went to the next form and repeated the same actions with a girl who looked to be a few years older than Neall. Ronan did not recognize her as Mountain Folk. She turned and looked at Granny with eyebrows raised, but Granny shook her head. She did not recognize the girl either. Did that mean that children had been taken from more villages than they knew?

The woman took each child by the hand and led them toward the entrance to the cave. Ronan could see them clearly in the dim light that entered from the outside. The woman stroked their hair and murmured to them over and over again. Their eyes were open, but there was no light behind them. No smiles or frowns crossed their faces, no expression at all. It was as if they were still sleeping, but with eyes wide open. Granny took Ronan by the hand again, and together they moved a few feet closer to the entrance, where they could hear the woman.

"You are to go to the valley, and there you will find a village with a bell tower in the square. Once there, you will look across the square and find the inn. It is easy to find because it is the only building made of stone. Once there, you will find the back stairs and go up, and you must be invisible. Invisible, I command. Go upstairs and try the doors. Find one that is open and go inside. There will be packs hanging on the hooks on the wall or in the cupboards. Take them down and look through them. Find sacks of coins, anything that shines, and put it in your pockets. Go down the hall and look for another door that is open. Look under the bed and through the room. Anything of value, put it in your pockets. Do not let anyone hear you or see you. If anyone comes in the room while you are there, hide in the cupboard or under the bed. Leave down the back stairs. Do not let anyone see you. Sleep in the stable until morning and then come back here at first light. Do not let anyone in the village see you leaving."

She continued to stroke their hair as she spoke. The children did not acknowledge her in any way, but as soon as she said, "Now go!" they turned and left.

Granny slipped farther back into the cave as the woman turned. Once more, the sound of her gown sweeping the cave floor was the only sound they heard. As she passed their hiding space, she stopped and stood still for just a moment. Ronan held her breath and squeezed Granny's hand. The woman walked on, and she let the air out in a rush. Granny pulled her hand sharply and put her fingers to her lips once more.

A clear, hard voice rang out from the back of the cave. "Oh, Granny Matilda, do not for a second think that I do not know you are there. And what's this? You've brought a friend this time. Tell me, Granny, are you slipping, that you need to bring company when you come to call on us? Let me see, who do you have here?"

Suddenly the woman stood right before them, black eyes flashing. "Oh, I see. Mountain Folk, is it? So, you have discovered that the Mountain Folk share some of your gifts?" She reached out a white hand and grabbed Ronan's arm. Ice ran up and down her arm, and she had to put her hand to her mouth to keep from crying out.

Granny reached out and calmly removed the woman's hand from Ronan's arm. "Now, now, Mara, you don't want to be doing that. You know I have powers beyond traveling, and you do not want to tempt me into using them now. Let her go, I say."

The woman she called Mara took a step back, rubbing the arm that Granny had touched as if it hurt her. "Have I underestimated you, old woman? Could it be that you know things I did not know you did? It matters not. You come back here again, and I will let you see the full power that I possess. I am able to call up things that will turn your heart to stone. How do you think I have these children here? You don't think Jebez and I carry them here, do you? I can call things forth that you would never recognize."

"Oh, I think I know how you've come to have these dear children. But I also think there is one more child that you crave. Am I right, Mara? Is there one more that you need?"

Mara drew back and looked at Granny through eyes closed to a narrow slit. "I don't know what you're talking about, old woman. I have all the children I need. I send them forth as often as I want, and they bring me what I need. They are my own little army of soldiers, and I alone direct them."

"Perhaps I am wrong, then, Mara. Perhaps you have all you need. But I think there is a reason you took my granddaughter, Tilly, and I do not believe it has anything to do with me."

The woman paused and looked at Granny thoughtfully. She closed her eyes for a moment, and Granny could feel her probing for answers, searching for something in Granny's mind. "You are dreaming, Granny. You don't have anything that I need or want. Whatever you think you have, remember that I gave it up years ago. Gave it up willingly, at that, Granny Matilda! Now go from here and do not come back, or I swear I will let loose Ceobhran, and we shall see how you fare with that!" She turned on her heels and swept away.

Granny pulled Ronan out of the cave on feet that seemed made of wood. Once outside, she reached up and closed Ronan's eyes and whispered, "Now think of Cormac and home. Think hard, concentrate on his face, his voice, his touch."

Ronan opened her eyes and saw Cormac sitting across from her, hands on his knees, staring at her so intently she gasped. Tears rolled down her face, and she held out her arms. Without a word, he leaped from his bench and gathered her up into his. She laid her head against his shoulder and wept softly. He patted her back and looked questioningly at Granny.

When Ronan caught her breath and tears stopped running down her face, he relaxed his hold on her but continued to sit beside her and hold her hand. "Oh, Granny, I have never felt such evil in my life. I have faced bear and mountain lion, but I have never been so full of fear as I was just now. And you talked to her as if you had a heart of steel. And oh, those children! Our children!" She hung her head and shook it softly back and forth.

"Granny, did you find Tilly? Did you see her?" demanded Conor.

"No, dear child, the children all have some sort of cloth draped over them, but she is there. I felt such a strong tug from her heart to mine that there is no question that she is there, Conor."

Granny sat back against the rock and closed her eyes. "Let me have a moment to clear my head, and then we will tell you what we saw."

22

SECRETS

Cormac addressed both the women, "Do we need to call Aelf and Shaen to hear this?"

Ronan answered for them both, "Yes, Cormac. And then he can decide if he wants to call a meeting of the council to hear it or not."

Cormac turned to Conor. "Would you do me a friend's favor, Conor, and go to Aelf's dwelling and bring him and Shaen? I don't want Ronan and Granny to have to tell the story more than they need to do. It will be bad enough telling it once."

Conor jumped to his feet and called to Wolf, and together they headed down the path that took them back to the Mountain Folk village.

Ronan gently pulled her hand out of Cormac's grasp and looked at him kindly. "I think I will fix us all some tea and check on Erik. Will you help me carry it out, please, Cormac?" She did not wait for his answer but got up and went through the doorway into her dwelling, with Cormac close behind.

Once inside, she bent over Erik Tamen, who was sleeping soundly. Turning, she began to gather up the utensils to brew tea. Cormac stirred her coals and fed some small sticks into them. He blew softly on them until a flame leaped out and began licking at the stack of wood.

Ronan continued to busy herself with the tea and did not look Cormac in the eyes. "Granny wanted someone to wait here that I cared about. Someone who could pull me back if I got lost out there or was too frightened to remember what to do. You were that person, Cormac. And it worked. She told me to picture you in my mind, hear your voice in my ear, and feel the touch of your hand. I did those things and felt myself pulled back here to where you sat waiting for me." All this was said softly while she gathered her dishes.

Cormac sat back on his heels by the fire and looked at her. "Ronan, I have cared for you for so long, but you are the Mountain Folk healer, and I am nothing. I never thought we would be anything more than friends."

"You are not nothing, Cormac!" Ronan's whispered voice rang sharp and clear. "You are respected in so many ways for your skill with a carving knife, your patience teaching the young folk, and your knowledge of our history. You are kind and good, and anyone would be honored to share your life."

Cormac was speechless. Never in all his days did he reckon that Ronan would consider him as a worthy suitor. And yet, she did! His heart sang and eyes glistened with unshed tears. Ronan brought the tea and the utensils to the fire and sat beside him. Together, they poured water and lifted rocks from the fire to drop into the pot until steam began to drift toward the roof of her cave. They did not say another word, but their hands touched as they poured the tea into cups, and when that happened, they smiled at one another.

When they brought the tea out, Cormac held the blanket aside so that Ronan could pass, and as she did, he lightly touched her shoulder. She turned and smiled at him, and he smiled back.

Granny observed this through half-open eyes from where she rested against the rock. *So, I guessed rightly,* she thought. *Good! That's one thing settled!*

As Ronan and Cormac were bringing the tea out, Aelf and Shaen came around the corner, Aelf practically bristling with impatience. Cormac handed him a cup of tea, and he sat down on a bench, with Shaen beside him.

"Well? What did you two see?" he demanded. Shaen gently put her hand on his forearm and nodded toward the cup in his hand. He looked down at it as if he had no idea how it came to be there. Blinking, he turned to Shaen, who smiled and nodded her head toward Cormac. "Oh, thank you for the tea, Brother. I appreciate it. Now, tell me what happened."

Ronan sat next to Cormac and turned her attention to Aelf. "We will tell you all that happened, Aelf."

Chastened, he murmured an apology toward Ronan and sat back to wait impatiently.

Ronan looked to Granny, who opened her eyes and smiled at Shaen and Aelf. "The first thing that I will tell you is that Neall is alive and there in the cave. And if he is there, I believe your other sons are there as well. That's the first thing you need to know."

Shaen gripped Aelf's hand and bowed her head. She took in a deep breath and sat back. "Thank you for that, Matilda! Now, please tell us what else you saw."

Granny started slowly, so that she wouldn't leave out any important detail, "There is a cave at the top of the highest peak. The peak is the one with the clouds around the top of it, it is so tall. But these are not ordinary clouds. They are made of something I am not sure of, but I believe they play a part in this trouble. Ronan and I went into the cave together. There we saw the same thing that I saw before: shapes covered with cloth. How many, do you think, Ronan?"

Ronan shook her head. "I lost count in the dark, Matilda. I think I counted over fifty, though. It seems like so many. So very many!"

Granny looked at her with sorrow. "Ronan, tell them what you saw, what you felt."

Ronan shuddered and then straightened her shoulders. "There was a woman there, a tall woman with long, black hair. Her hair fell down her back in waves. If there had been light in the cave, I think it would have shone like the feathers of a raven, but with no light, it was like coal. She was dressed in black, some heavy material that I don't know about. It looked soft, yet it rustled against the floor of the cave when she walked by. The sound of it raised the hair on the back of my neck for some reason, and it felt as if pure evil had walked past us. I think if I had reached out to touch her, my hand would have come back frozen, as if I had stuck it down deep in a snowbank."

Again, Ronan shuddered, but she quickly gathered herself. "She was touching the shapes as she walked past them, talking to them as if they were wee babes and she was putting them to sleep. She came to one and bent down to speak to the shape, and when she did, she pulled back the cloth and the figure sat up. It was Neall! Oh, Shaen, how I wanted to call out to him. How I wanted to rouse him from this sleep he is in, but Granny held me tight, and I did not. The woman woke another figure, this time a girl, and she took them by the hand and led them to the cave entrance. There, she gave them instructions, and they left to carry them out. What was horrible was that there was no life in these poor creatures. They stood, they listened, they nodded their heads, but there were no words from their mouths, no light in their eyes. It was as if they were walking in their sleep."

"What sort of instructions?" Aelf demanded.

Granny answered him, "She sent them down to the village, our village, Conor. She told them to go to the inn and search through the rooms for anything of value. They were to spend the night in the stable and return to her in the morning with whatever they found. I can only imagine that she would not be pleased if they came back empty-handed."

Shaen gasped. "She is turning my Neall into a thief?"

"Yes, Shaen, she is. As children, they would not arouse suspicion, and she is sending them to villages other than their own so that they won't be recognized. I don't know how often she sends them, or what she does with the things they bring back."

"Matilda, how does she wake them? You said they are sleeping, but she says something and they sit up and walk. What does she say to get them to do that?"

"I don't know, Shaen, not yet. I am going to have to go back and try to learn that. And I must hide much better next time."

Ronan shook her head. "I don't think you should go back, Matilda. I heard what that awful woman said to you. How she threatened you."

All heads swiveled back to face Granny. They all spoke at once with the same concern written across their faces. "You spoke to her? She spoke to you?"

Granny looked hard at Ronan and shook her head in an almost imperceptible manner. Ronan frowned but said no more.

"Yes, she knew we were there. How, I'm not sure, but she knew. She looked right at us and spoke to us. She told me that she could call up Ceobhran. I suspect that is how she has our children."

"What in all that is holy is Ceobhran?" growled Aelf. "I've never heard of this person. Who is it, and what does he have to do with all of this?"

"It is not a person, Aelf. It is a thing, a thing that, in the far past, people tried to control. It is something out of children's stories that parents told to frighten them into behaving. 'Watch out, or Ceobhran will come for you!' That sort of thing. I heard of it from my grandmother and my mother, but I thought it was just stories, made up. My grandma told me that in the old days, people used incantations or something like that to bring up Ceobhran to do their bidding. I never believed the stories, never had any reason to, but now it begins to make sense to me how so many of our children could disappear right from under our noses and we never caught a whiff of anything."

Conor shook his head. "I still don't understand, Granny. How does this Ceobhran get our children? How did it get Tilly?"

"Oh, Conor, I wish I knew exactly, but I don't. I am trying to remember the stories that they told to me, but it's been years, and I'm afraid they are vague in my memory. I just remember that people would try to call up this thing and learn to command it to do any sort of thing that they couldn't do themselves. And it still doesn't explain how the children are sleeping and how she is able to wake them. There is so much more we need to learn, I'm afraid."

Cormac added his voice to the discussion. "How do you plan on doing that, Matilda? You are planning on returning, aren't you?"

"I have no choice, Cormac. How else will we learn what we need to get the children? And no, Ronan, I think I will do this alone. It could be that by going alone, I will have a better chance of sneaking in undetected. At any rate, I am not willing to risk you another time. When I have the knowledge that we need, then we can go together, I promise."

Granny got up from her seat and, without another word, went into Ronan's dwelling, carrying her empty teacup. Ronan followed and, leaning against the wall, folded her arms and looked sternly at Granny. "What is going on, Matilda? First of all, if you think for a moment that I am going to let you go up to that cave by yourself, you are wrong. What kind of friend would I be if I did that? And second, why the look outside? What is it that you didn't want me to say?"

Granny smiled at Ronan. "If there was anyone more in touch with me than you, Ronan, I'm not sure who it would be, other than my dear Tilly. And yes, you are right, there was something I didn't want you to say. I can't explain it right now, but I know you heard me call the woman by name. You would do me a very big service if you would forget that name. Never mention it again. Someday, when this is all over, I promise I will tell you why, but for now, it must remain my secret. Do you agree to that?"

Ronan tilted her head to one side and looked speculatively at Granny. "Yes, but only if you agree that I will accompany you when you go back to the cave. I don't want you to go by yourself, Matilda."

Granny patted her hand and walked over to check on Erik Tamen. "Still sleeping, I see. That's all this man does now is eat and sleep, like a newborn babe. When will he be ready to travel, Ronan?"

"Oh, Matilda, I know he's getting stronger, but there still seems to be something wrong with his spirit. I'm not sure if it is his head injury or the injury to his pride that keeps him sleeping more than he should. He wakes, says a few words, eats like he has never eaten in his life, and then immediately falls back to sleep. Even when he talks, he doesn't say much. He seems deeply troubled by something, but he won't confide in me, so I cannot help him. I wish there was someone who could talk to him."

"I have an idea, Ronan. Erik has been our leader for many years now. Everyone in the village depended on him and looked up to him. I believe he feels as if he has let us all down, first with the disappearance of our children and then his failure to bring them back home to us."

"That's ridiculous, Matilda! After what I've seen up there, no one could have known this would happen or been able to stop it. Are you thinking that perhaps Aelf could reach out to him, Matilda?"

"Oh, you are good, my friend. Yes, I think one leader to another might make a difference to Erik. Perhaps Aelf could help him see that it is not his fault. I will ask him to come talk with Erik if you think it's a good idea."

"I do, and I hope it helps him."

"I will ask him to come after evening meal. Perhaps you could see that Erik sits outside for a while after he eats?"

"Of course. Thank you, Matilda, for taking me seriously." Granny patted her hand again and rose to leave.

Conor and Wolf followed Cormac back to his dwelling. The boy had found a much-needed friend and confidant in Cormac. While he had always looked up to Erik Tamen, Cormac was someone he could talk with and feel as if he was heard for the first time. He found he had so much inside him to pour out to Cormac that, at times, he was embarrassed by how much he confided in the older man. Cormac was a good listener and would nod and ask questions occasionally but never interrupt or grow impatient. Conor had even shared that he was an orphan, at least as far as he knew.

Cormac couldn't imagine what it must have felt like to have your parents disappear in the middle of the night with no explanation. He admired the way Conor refused to be taken in by the villagers, preferring to live in the meager little cottage that he claimed for himself. He asked Conor to describe it to him, and he listened while Conor spoke with pride about the repairs he had made and the neatness of his home. How on this green earth he had managed to survive on his own was a small miracle, but to have done so without being bitter was an even greater miracle. He more than understood how Conor would prefer animals to most people, with the exception of Matilda and her granddaughter, Tilly.

Now, there was a light in his eye if ever Cormac had seen one when Conor talked about Tilly. His face fairly shone with the love he bore that girl. Cormac wondered if he knew just how much he loved Tilly. Maybe it was something that someone else had to point out to you, like the way that Matilda had let him know that he was important to Ronan. Oh, how he'd felt when he learned that! There were no words to describe the feeling of relief knowing that his feelings for her were returned in full measure.

Granny found Aelf sitting with Shaen outside their home. They sat close and held each other's hands, talking softly. "I am so sorry to interrupt, but may I speak to you for just a moment, Aelf?"

Aelf brushed something away from his face and gestured to Granny to have a seat. "Shaen and I were just talking about our boys, Matilda. It is so good to know that you saw Neall, but we worry about all three of the boys. What is this woman turning them into? How will we get them back home? Will they ever be the same again? Oh, Matilda, our hearts are glad and sorrowful at the same time."

"I understand, I really do. Shaen, Aelf, I wish I could give you any kind of guarantee about the future for your children, but I can't. I can say this, though with no proof beyond seeing your youngest: I think all three of your children are alive. I don't know yet how we will wake them and bring them home, but I will do my best to learn as much as I can. In my heart, I feel that if we can get them away from that woman, we can restore them to their true selves once again."

"Matilda, why do I have the sense that you know that woman?" Shaen looked at Granny directly, without blinking or moving her gaze.

"Because I do, Shaen, but please believe me when I say that I have my reasons for keeping her a secret right now. If you could and would trust me, my heart would be lighter."

"Of course we trust you. It was a curiosity more than anything. I was just wondering if my feeling was right. What did you need to talk with us about, Matilda?"

"It is Aelf I need to ask a favor of. The favor is for Erik. Ronan thinks there is damage to his spirit, Aelf. I don't know, but I think she might be right. I think he has suffered because, as our leader, it was his job to keep us safe, and barring that, it was his job to right the wrong against our village. You are a leader here, Aelf, and have been for as long or more than Erik has in our village. I wonder if, as a leader, you could talk with him, get him to confide in you? I think it might help him to know that you also suffer from the loss of your children and have felt helpless to do anything until now. Would you do that for me?"

Aelf looked at the ground between his feet and frowned. Admitting that he had failed to a stranger, especially a lowlander? How could he do that? Yes, he felt as if he had let down his people, but was that something that you talked about with a stranger? He'd barely confided his feelings to Shaen, and now this woman wanted him to talk with a lowlander? Aelf scuffed his foot back and forth and watched the path it made in the dirt.

Granny sat puzzled at his silence and looked questioningly at Shaen. Had she missed something? What was his reluctance?

Aelf raised his head and looked at Granny. "It is very hard to be a leader and feel the failure that I have felt this past many seasons. It is hard to see the pain and the questions in the eyes of the Mountain Folk and not have any answers for them. It is hard to admit you have failed. I know. And yes, this lowlander might feel the same way. It will be hard for me to talk with him, but I will try."

"Oh, Aelf, I did not consider how difficult it might be for you to do this. Please forgive me. I was only thinking of myself and my village. I thank you with all my heart for trying. I will not forget what you are willing to do for us."

Shaen got up from her seat to walk Granny down the path. "We will do what we can to help Erik heal. I believe you are going to go back up to the cave, Matilda. Am I right in this thinking?"

"I have no choice, Shaen. I must know how to wake the children. I don't want us to try to control them down the mountain. I want them fully awake and able to help each other, help the young ones, because I do believe there are young ones among them."

"You believe this woman is sending these children out to steal for her?"

"I honestly think she sends them to do more than that, but I have no proof of that, so I am not willing to say. But, yes, I think she sends them to steal and possibly much more. Children are so often overlooked. They are able to slip into places without notice, walk through crowds without attracting attention, and do more in the background than you or I could ever hope to do, simply because people often don't look at children the same way that they look at us. I think this woman has found the perfect group of little soldiers for herself, and our job is to see that there is an end to this."

"Matilda, there is something else that I noticed when you and Ronan were describing what you saw there. I am sure I am wrong, but I thought for just a moment you were warning Ronan not to say something. For just a moment, I thought I saw you shake your head ever so slightly. Now, it seems to me that you were determined to tell us everything. That there should be no more secrets between the lowlanders and the Mountain Folk, so it troubles me to think these thoughts. What do you say to this?"

Granny was silent for a moment and then, taking Shaen's hand, led her to a seat far away from the entrance to her home. Sitting on a log bench, she took both of Shaen's hands in hers and looked her in the eyes. "My dear friend, you have taken us in and treated us like family. You have put aside differences that your tribe has held on to for generations so that we might work together for the common good. You have not questioned me or Conor but have taken everything on our word. We could not have asked for more from the Mountain Folk. And yes, there is something that I keep to myself, but I am not keeping it from you. The truth is, I know something that might break someone's heart, someone I care deeply for. This in no way affects you or what we are going to do, but the thought of this small piece of knowledge finding its way out in the open is a problem I have not been able to work out in my mind. Please trust me that that is all it is. A desire to protect someone that I care for."

Shaen said nothing, just squeezed Granny's hand and walked back to her dwelling.

23

THE WORDS

Granny and Conor shared the evening meal with Shaen and Aelf: two different kinds of roasted meat seasoned with wild onions and garlic; wild rice cooked soft with pine nuts and dried berries, then rolled into balls and fried in fat; a flatbread made from ground nuts and cooked on flat rocks until it was soft and warm; all washed down with a warm, honey-flavored drink that made Conor's head a little fuzzy. Granny helped Shaen clean the utensils and stack them back on the rock shelves in her dwelling.

Then they all sat around an outside fire and traded stories about their lives. Conor listened to Aelf's stories of hunting in the mountains, tracking deer and bear, waiting until the right moment to let loose his arrows, sometimes tracking a wounded animal for hours before bringing back the meat to his village, where all the Folk shared it. Conor could imagine the pride in being able to bring food to the Mountain Folk. He wondered at the thrill of hunting and tracking an animal as big as a bear with only a few arrows and a good knife at your belt. The thought of the hours alone in the mountains and in the forest appealed to him. Solitude had always been Conor's friend, until he met Tilly. Now solitude seemed like a burden, because it was not his choice—it was forced on him by her absence.

The moon had risen by the time Granny said good night to Aelf and Shaen and asked Conor to walk her back to the cave that the Mountain Folk had generously provided them during their stay. Conor yawned widely and stretched his arms as they walked along the path. "That Shaen can cook. I never thought roasted game and wild rice could be so delicious, Granny. And that bread she made from grinding the nuts. I thought bread only came from good wheat. The Mountain Folk have learned a lot by being here by themselves, haven't they?"

"Yes, indeed, Conor. They've learned to take care of themselves, and that is by far the most important lesson, I think. I still wish they could come back to the valley and learn some of the things that we do. Their deer and bear skins might be soft, but there is nothing so good as a wool blanket at night or a good wool skirt to wear in the winter."

They arrived at their borrowed dwelling and entered through the door woven of cedar bark, finely shredded and worked until it was as soft as the deer skins that covered their sleeping platforms.

The front of the cave was a large, open room, where a fire pit constructed from flat rocks piled three high around a circle held the ashes from their morning fire. After morning meal, it had become their habit to spend the day with the Mountain Folk, Cormac or Ronan, and others. They took the midday meal and the evening meal with Aelf and Shaen, with Cormac often joining them. It was not until evening became night that they came back to their own dwelling.

From the front room, there was a narrow passageway that led to two separate chambers, one for each of them. A rock platform held the furs and hides that made up a soft bed, a wooden chest that held Granny's herbs and remedies, and one for Conor that held the treasures he had collected since arriving. In his chest, he kept his arrows and the bow that he was working to perfect, an extra pair of deer hide moccasins so soft that he was afraid to wear them over the rocks that scattered the paths around the village, and assorted pinecones and rocks that he had found. He hoped someday to share these things with Tilly. He could imagine the delight on her face when she held the moccasins and felt their softness. She would want him to show her how to shoot the arrows with his bow, and she would admire the rocks for their colors and shapes.

Wolf loved the cave, partly, Conor thought, because he was much like his namesake and the cave felt like home to him. The dog slept on a separate hide on the floor next to Conor's sleeping platform. There were two wooden bowls: one for water and one for his food. Conor always managed to slip a piece of meat or a handful of roasted grains into his pocket to feed Wolf at night. He knew the Mountain Folk had taken to Wolf and often saved tidbits for him to eat, but Conor liked the idea that he could feed his own dog every night before they slept. It gave him a good deal of satisfaction to watch Wolf's face as he cut up the meat and ground the grains in with it. Wolf would stare so intently Conor would laugh at him. "You know this is for you. Why do you worry?" he asked Wolf. Wolf's best reply was a small growl that came all the way up from his chest.

This evening, Granny asked Conor to join her in the front room when he finished feeding Wolf. "There's something I must do, and I fear I will need your help to do it."

Conor nodded and left to feed Wolf, returning after a few minutes. Granny was seated on one of the small benches carved from a cedar log, and she motioned for Conor to sit at the other.

"I need to go back up to the mountain cave, Conor. My goal is two things: I have to find out how they wake the children so that we can rouse them and lead them out of there. And I need to find out exactly where Tilly is. I think if we can wake her first, she might be able to help us wake the others. I fear that when we all get there, it will be wise for just one or two of us to enter the cave. The others must stay a good distance away, or we run the risk of discovery. If we are discovered, we as well as the children could be in danger, serious danger. The people who have taken the children mean to hold them at any cost. I believe after what Ronan and I saw, they mean to make a livelihood from these children, and that is not something they will give up easily.

"I am not certain what powers they hold, but I know they are able to call up Ceobhran and make it do their bidding. I am not clear what Ceobhran is capable of doing, but from the stories I have heard, you can't let it touch you. Once it touches you, you become it, and it becomes you, until it releases you. I believe that the children remain under its power and that the people have the words to wake them but not release them entirely. I need two things: the words to wake them and eventually the words to release them. I wonder if perhaps distance from Ceobhran will be the key to releasing them, but I cannot be sure until I observe the children for a time."

Conor looked at Granny without speaking. He rubbed his forehead and ran his fingers through his hair, brushing it away from his face. Finally, he spoke to her. "I understand what is at stake, Granny. Your life against the lives of the children. Am I right in this thinking?"

"I think that might be an exaggeration, Conor. I don't know where you got the idea that my life might be in danger by going there. I plan on sneaking in like a spider, hiding in the corners and watching and listening. No one will know that I am there."

"I think it was something Ronan said, or started to say, that made me think there was someone there who threatened you. I want the truth, Granny. Is there a threat to you?"

"Yes, Conor," she answered sadly. "The people there seem to have an uncanny sense that I am there. It's happened both times I went. The woman is able to find me no matter how careful I am. But I have no choice, Conor. And what I need is for you to be here as Cormac was for Ronan. If I should get in trouble there, I might need your pull to bring me back. With you thinking of me, thinking of us together, I have a north star to guide me home. Will you do it?"

Conor nodded. "Of course. There was no doubt in your mind. What should I look for, Granny? How can I help best?"

"Just be here. Keep me in your mind. Stay awake, stay alert, watch me for signs of distress. Don't touch me or speak to me, but if you think I am in trouble, call out to me in your mind only. Think as hard as you can about me, and I will hear you."

Granny leaned against the wall and let her hands drop softly to her lap. Her breathing became slow and regular, as if she had fallen asleep, but Conor knew she was awake, although in a different place.

The dirt outside the cave shifted and crunched under her feet. *Funny that I travel in my mind, but my body can still change things here,* Granny thought. She stood stock-still and felt the icy air from the cave wash over her body. She shivered with the cold and wrapped her cloak around her more tightly. One step at a time, she slowly advanced into the cave, hugging the wall to her left. Once inside, she stopped and let her eyes adjust to the gloom. There was a glow that flickered against the wall as if from a fire, the shadow it made changing shapes and growing larger and then smaller. She stood so still that her breath hardly moved her chest. Here she waited, waited for someone or something to come into the chamber. Her legs ached from standing, and her body shivered despite her woolen cloak. *I am too old for this,* she thought. She leaned slightly back to relieve the tension in her legs, bending them at the knees to keep them awake. She prayed that Conor would be able to stay awake, for she felt in her heart that she would need him before this night was through.

Her patience was rewarded with the sound of voices coming from a passageway at the far end of the chamber. She saw two shadows pass through the light of the fire, and then two forms entered. Mara of the raven's-wing black hair was followed by a bearded man with greasy, unkempt hair that straggled around his shoulders. His voice was muffled by the enormous beard that seemed to have swallowed half his face.

"Mara, we have a room full of gold and silver, enough candle-sticks to light half the town, and more silver bowls than we can ever eat out of. I am tired of living in this damp cave and sleeping on rocks. I wonder who is being punished here—them, or us, for having to live like this. I want to take what we have and go live where the sun shines and I can be warm again. Mara, wait! I want to talk about this!" the man's voice whined, rising to a near yell.

The woman he called Mara whirled to face him. As she did, he took a step or two backward in the face of her fury. "Enough, Jebez," she hissed. "We go when I say go, we go where I say to go, and we go how I say we go. I will not have you question me again. I want one more thing, and I think you know what it is. With this one more thing, we can take what we have and go, because we will have the means to get everything we need from then on. I know that wretched woman Matilda has what I need, and sooner or later, she will bring it to me. Then, and only then, will we leave here. Do you understand, Jebez?"

Jebez raised his hands to his throat and clawed at an invisible force around his neck. His eyes pleaded with Mara to stop, but no words left his tortured throat. He nodded, and immediately the tension around his neck loosened, and he could breathe again. "Mara, there is no need to hurt me. I just wanted to talk about leaving. I will be patient, I promise."

The man named Jebez followed meekly behind Mara as she turned on her heel and walked toward the chamber. Her black gown swept the floor and made a soft rustling sound as she approached a child sleeping on a stone platform.

She raised a white hand and pulled back the cloth that covered the face. She stared down at the sleeping girl and smiled to herself, a slow smile that touched her lips but not her eyes. Her eyes, black as the night, glittered in the pale light. Slowly, she brushed the girl's hair away from her face, her hand lingering across her cheek as if in a caress.

Granny shivered to watch Mara stroke the sleeping child. She straightened her knees and craned silently to see the child asleep before Mara. A gasp nearly escaped her lips, for she saw Tilly, her own sweet Tilly, on the platform. Covering her mouth with her hand, she stifled the cry that threatened to escape. Tears coursed down Granny's wrinkled cheeks, making a path as they did. She dared not move even to brush them away but stood so still that she could hear her own heartbeat in her ears.

Mara continued to stroke the girl, fanning her hair around her head, murmuring softly. "It's your turn, my dear. Your turn to bring me something valuable. Ceobhran, awake this child. Ceobhran, allow me to have this child now. *Eirich, eirich ainmhi baineann. Eirich e cogar, ainmhi baineann.* Arise and listen, girl!"

Tilly sat up on the platform and swung her feet to the floor. Her eyes were open, but there was no light behind them. She stared straight ahead and never looked at Mara or acknowledged her in any way. Mara continued to stroke her soft blonde hair, unbound from the braid that usually hung down her back. "You will go out and hunt for me tonight, child. You will go to the village at the far north end of the valley. It will take you this night and all the next day to reach it. When you do, you will enter the largest house on the square. It is a stone house that has been whitewashed and newly thatched. There is a door in the back that lets into the kitchen. There you will find the cook and her helper. You will go in and ask for food. When they give it to you, you will sit and eat it all, and you will smile and thank them for it.

"When they turn their backs, you will slip from the kitchen into the passageway that takes you to the main house. There you will find the stairs that lead up to the sleeping quarters. Go into the largest room. It will have a cupboard with clothes hanging in it. Behind the clothes, there will be a box covered in velvet. Open the box and take everything out of it. Here is a pouch that you will fill with the contents of the box. Tie it to your skirt and hide it under your cloak so no one sees it. Slip back down the stairs and leave by the side door. Do not go back to the kitchen. They will think you have gone after your meal and will not look for you, but if they see you, they will question you. You must not be seen by anyone. Travel the night and the next day and bring me back the things that you found." Mara pressed a good-sized pouch into Tilly's hand. "Now go, child. Go!"

Granny watched helplessly as Tilly walked toward the entrance to the cave, passing within an arm's length of where she stood. Oh, how she wanted to reach out and grab her, shake her until her senses returned, and then run like the devil himself away from this hideous place. But no, she must wait until she was sure of how to awaken the children.

Mara stood thoughtfully watching Tilly walk away. "Jebez, I do not trust that one. She has the strongest will of any of the children. I am afraid she will not carry out my commands. I believe I will send my own safeguard to make sure she does."

Mara moved through the sleeping bodies, trailing her hand across them as she glided past. She reached the end of the second row of children and stopped, looking thoughtfully at the sleeping shape before her. "Yes, this one will do quite nicely. He has proven to be loyal, and I believe he will do whatever it is I ask of him."

She lifted the cloth from the body to reveal a young boy, perhaps a year or so older than Tilly. His face was hard and lean, with little boyhood look to it. She moved the hair from across his forehead and bent down close to his ear. "*Eirich, eirich e cogar, ogfhear*. Arise, arise and listen, boy."

As with before, the boy sat up and swung his feet over the edge of the sleeping platform. Once again, no light was visible in the child's eyes. He sat still, eyes staring straight ahead, seeing nothing. Mara put both her hands on the side of his face and breathed into his face, once, twice, three times. "*Ackman, ackman, Ceobhran*. Release him to me."

The boy's eyes shifted from the cave wall to Mara's face, and for an instant, there was no recognition. Then a smile crossed his face and he reached up to hold her arms with his hands. "Mother, have I been sleeping again?"

"Yes, dear boy, but I have need of you now. I want you to listen closely and obey me. Will you do that?"

"Yes, Mother. Haven't I always done what you've asked of me? Haven't I proved my worth to you over and over? Send me out, and I will do whatever you need."

"Good, I hoped I could count on you. There is a girl, Tilly is her name. I have sent her to the village at the farthest end of the valley, to the home of the mayor. I want you to follow her, but I do not want you to interfere with her. I need to know if she follows my commands. Watch her, make sure she goes to the stone house, newly white-washed. Do not follow her inside but wait outside for her. When she comes out, see if she is carrying anything, and then follow her back here. I want to know if she stops to talk with anyone, if she meets anyone, or if she does anything to arouse suspicion in any way. Do you understand?"

"Perfectly." The boy stood and kissed the woman on the cheek and moved toward the cave entrance.

Granny stared from the darkness of the wall she hugged tightly in an effort to make herself as small as possible. She dared not breathe, but her heart sang with the knowledge she now had. She had the words to awaken the children! She had watched Mara and listened to every word she said, watched every gesture the woman made. Ever so slightly, she moved one foot and then another backward, still hugging the wall, her hands gripping her wool skirt tightly. All she had to do was creep out of the darkness the same way she crept in, one foot at a time, just like the spider, unseen and unheard.

Without warning, a hand gripped her arm just above the elbow, wrenching it backward and causing her to catch her breath with the pain of it.

A harsh voice rasped in her ear, "What have I found here? A rat? A sneaking, filthy rat of a woman?" Granny was spun around to meet a heavily bearded face, with long, black hair, matted and dirty. She recoiled from the smell of his breath as much as the pain in her arm.

"Let go of me, Jebez. Now!" Granny's voice, though clear, was barely above a whisper. She pulled her arm from his grasp, rubbing it to bring back the feeling.

Jebez reached out to grab her again, but this time he met resistance, resistance he could not see but could feel blocking his hand from touching Granny. "I know you, old woman! Aren't you that meddling old woman from the valley? Aren't you the one they say can see the future? You have a power I did not know you had, old woman. But it won't do you any good here. Mara will call up Ceobhran, and you will be as these children are, asleep and ours for as long as we choose to keep you alive."

Once more, he reached for Granny, this time meaning to grab the long gray braid that fell to the middle of her back. Granny closed her eyes tightly and thought of Conor. *Oh please, Conor, think of me now. Hear me calling you. Hold me in your mind.*

Granny twisted away from Jebez's grasp and scurried down the row of sleeping platforms. Jebez darted after her, his heavy boots echoing on the cave floor. Just as he reached out to grab her, she became as mist, and his hand fell through the empty air.

Granny's eyes flew open, and she stared at Conor across from her. His face was white as death, and his fists were clenched at his sides. She looked at him and smiled, and his hands relaxed. She could see the tension leave his face. "I am back, Conor. Thank you for helping me return." She leaned against the wall, looking frail and tired. "I am back, and I know what to do!"

24

CEOBHRAN

C onor left his bench to sit next to Granny. "What happened? I could feel something awful happening to you, and your body twitched and seemed to want to get up and run. I didn't touch you, Granny, but it was the hardest thing I've had to do in a while. All I could do was sit here and watch you and concentrate."

"Oh, Conor, it was the best thing you could do for me. I did get myself into a bit of trouble up there. It was going so well, and I was on my way out of the cave, when I was caught by the man. It's hard to explain, but it's best to travel to and from safe places. The cave is not safe, so I wanted to get outside to travel back to you. For some reason, it is so much harder to leave a dangerous place than a safe one. With your guidance, I was able to come back."

"What did you find out, Granny? Did you find Tilly? Is she all right? Were you able to find anything that will help us?"

"Yes, I found Tilly. In fact, she is the one who helped me find the words we will need to rouse the children. The woman woke her, but of course, she is not really awake. It is like she is sleepwalking. She hears and obeys without question. Poor Tilly, to be abused so. She would never do the things they make her do if she were awake and in charge of herself. It broke my heart to see that woman use her, Conor.

It was all I could do not to rush out and grab her and jerk her away. I couldn't, you know. I hope you understand why."

"Oh, Granny, you saw her? You saw our Tilly? I want her back so much, it hurts." Conor hung his head with the sorrow he carried. Granny put her arm around his shoulder, and for a moment they sat still together, both thinking of Tilly.

Conor took a deep breath and sat up straight. "Tell me what you found up there, Granny," he demanded.

Granny sighed and sat back to touch the wall behind her. "Don't suppose it can wait until tomorrow?" she asked.

Conor said nothing, but the look he gave Granny spoke all the words he needed to convince her.

"I heard the words the woman issues to wake them. They are ancient words, Conor, words I had never heard spoken aloud. I recognize them only because of some very old writings I have from my grandmother's grandmother. In it, she warns that these are powerful words that deal with the specter Ceobhran. Ceobhran is like a mist, a fog, perhaps, that can be used to do your bidding if you know the ancient words to control it."

Granny looked off into the distance, as if she could see the ancient text in front of her. "The man said that she could call it up, and if it touched me, I would become it and it would become me. That makes sense for the manner in which the children sleep and how they act when it appears they are awake. They are controlled by Ceobhran. I heard the words she used to rouse Tilly, and then she sent her to steal for her. Oh, Conor, it broke my heart. My good, sweet Tilly doing the bidding of this horrible woman. To be controlled by her!" Granny put her hand on her chest and sat quietly for a moment.

Conor did not interrupt to question her further. He knew she would finish when she was able.

Granny sat up and began again. "I heard more than that, Conor. The woman sent a boy to spy on Tilly. She was afraid that Tilly would not follow her commands. I believe she said something about Tilly being strong-willed." Granny laughed at that. "Imagine! Tilly, strong-willed! What I heard next was more important than ever. I heard the words that allowed the boy to be released from Ceobhran's grip. He was fully awake and could speak of his own accord. She sent him after Tilly, but only to watch her and bring back word of her actions to the woman."

This time it was Conor who rested his head against the wall and closed his eyes. "We know how to get them back, Granny. You are so brave to have gone there, not once but three times. You dared risk your life for the children, for Tilly most of all. Now how do we use this to free them?"

"I think I need some rest now, but in the morning, we will talk with Erik and Aelf and anyone else from the Mountain Folk who wants to be heard. We will have to make a plan, Conor, one that keeps us safe and frees the children. And most importantly, we must wait for Tilly's return. The woman sent her to a village that is at the farthest reach of the valley, so figuring the trip to be about two full days and nights, we must wait that long. I want Tilly to be there to help us, and it occurred to me that she can only be released while she is in the cave. I have no proof of that, just a very strong feeling. But for now, I must rest. This night has taken a toll on an old woman. I hope you will forgive me my age and frailty."

Conor laughed and patted her hand. "Nothing frail or old about you, Granny Matilda. I am glad that Tilly is named for you. She will need the strength of that good name before this is over. First thing after morning meal, we will go see Erik and tell him the news."

Conor surprised Granny by having a morning meal all prepared when she came out of her sleeping room. The fire was still warm and the prepared food was laid out on flat rocks around the fire to keep it warm for eating. Cakes made of grains, nuts, and fruit were baked alongside strips of meat cooked in fat. Hot tea steamed in cups near the fire. Conor handed her a wooden plate and utensil as soon as she sat down.

"This looks and smells delicious, Conor. Where did you learn to make all this?"

"I've been watching you and Shaen and Ronan cook since we arrived. It didn't seem too hard, and I wanted to try my hand at it." He chewed some of the meal before grinning at Granny. "The meat is a little tough! Watch your teeth on the cakes. I think I might have missed a shell from the nuts."

"It is wonderful and much appreciated!"

They finished their meal in silence and drank their tea outside in the early morning sun. Conor tried not to show his impatience as Granny drank her tea and stared at the mountain in the distance. Finally, she put her cup aside and turned to Conor.

"I have been thinking, Conor, of the best way to approach this problem. I know that the men, Erik and Aelf, will be impatient to rush into the cave and start snatching up children, but that would be disastrous. I believe the best thing is to sneak in and quietly wake the children, a few at a time, and send them out to where you and the rest of the Mountain Folk wait for them. Let them start taking the children down the mountain to safety while I stay in the cave and continue to release them. I know you are going to want to be in there with me, but I think it's important that you and Tilly work together to get as many to safety as possible. Do you agree to this?"

Conor looked at Granny thoughtfully. "Why do I always have this feeling you are keeping something from me, Granny? I can't figure out what it could possibly be, but I still have a strong sense. Is it about Tilly? Do you think she will be changed by this experience?"

"Conor, I promise, anything I keep from you is only for your own good. And yes, Tilly might be changed by this. I don't know what lingering effects there might be from having Ceobhran control you. I cannot think that it will not leave a mark on her, as well as the other children. But you're ignoring my request, Conor. Do you agree to wait outside the cave and help with the children?"

"Yes, Granny, of course. I don't like the idea of you facing that man and woman alone, but I understand that most of us need to be there to help the children get away safely. I think they're going to be confused and scared. Most of them are not going to recognize any of us, and that's going to make it harder to gain their trust. I will do my best to calm them and reassure them that we are taking them to their homes again."

"That's settled, then. Let's find Aelf and Shaen and meet with the others. Do me a friend's favor and find Ronan and Cormac and ask them to join us. If Erik is with Ronan, he must come as well. I think there might be a chance he is talking with Aelf, but if you see him first, ask him to meet us in the council area."

Granny left to find Aelf and Shaen, with Conor seeking out his good friend Cormac. When he and Cormac found Ronan, she was busy cleaning up after morning meal. "Granny is ready to meet with all of us. She knows how to wake the children. Ronan, it's finally time to go!"

Ronan put down the dishes she was cleaning and fixed Conor and Cormac with a fierce stare. "She went back to the cave, didn't she? I told her that I wanted to go with her. I didn't think it was safe for her to go alone. Was she all right?"

Conor shook his head. "Not entirely. The woman didn't find her out, but there is a man there, and he found her. He tried to hold her for the woman, but Granny slipped away. She asked me to sit with her, like Cormac did for you when you went with her. It helped, she said."

Ronan blushed at the memory of Cormac pulling her back from the cave with his will power. "The fates take her, Matilda will be the death of us all, those of us who love her, which I imagine is just about all of us!" Ronan put her dishes on the shelves and followed Cormac and Conor out of her dwelling.

"I don't see Erik around. Do you know where he is?" asked Conor.

"He went for a walk with Aelf. Aelf came over just after morning meal and asked Erik to walk with him. I think he wanted to talk with Erik about the difficulty of being a leader. Aelf should know about that. He's suffered a lot in this past year, knowing he was helpless to find our children. I suspect that Erik is carrying a burden of guilt himself. Maybe, just maybe, Aelf can help him put some of that burden aside."

They walked together to the council area, the large amphitheater carved from the side of the mountain. The benches reserved for council members were nearly full when they arrived, and the Mountain Folk were filling the benches facing them. Everyone was quiet and subdued; there were no greetings echoing across the area, no laughter or backslapping this morning. People filed in and sat quietly, facing the council benches.

Aelf took his place with the council members, and Maeve, who had called the meeting to order when they last met to discuss the problem of Erik Tamen, rose once more and rapped her staff sharply on the ground, once, twice, three times.

There was no need to call for order; not a sound was heard, and all eyes were focused only on the council. Maeve turned to look at Aelf. "I do not know the extent of what has happened, and therefore, I am not able to speak to the Folk. Are you able to do so, Aelf?"

Aelf stood and bowed in respect to Maeve. "I have bits and pieces, Maeve, but the person who knows the whole story is Matilda, the lowlander. She has the gift of travel; some of you know this because she has been working with you. I gather Ronan also possesses the gift to some degree. Matilda and Ronan traveled to the cave where our children are being held, and she traveled there again on her own last night. I am going to let her explain everything to you."

The Mountain Folk sat silently, but hands were clasped with loved ones, tears shone in their eyes, and some put their arms around others and allowed heads to rest on their shoulders. Granny walked to the edge of the raised platform, where the council occupied their benches. She folded her hands and looked out on the Folk.

"It's true. We saw some of the children, Ronan and I. We saw Neall." An audible gasp was heard from the Folk, and all eyes turned to look at Shaen. Those near her reached out to touch her shoulder, squeeze her arm, pat her in support.

Granny continued, "I did go back last night for two reasons. I needed to find out if my Tilly was there; you will forgive an old woman her selfishness. And I needed to find a way to wake them. Your children slumber, but it is not the sleep of innocence. It is the troubled sleep of those controlled by a force that we cannot see and cannot fight. They are awakened and sent out into the world to do the bidding of the woman who controls them. I needed the words to wake them, and even more than that, I needed the words to free them from the force that holds them so tightly. I have those words. I watched as the woman roused my dear Tilly and then woke a boy to follow her. Now, I think, we should consider how best to bring them all home."

Granny stood to one side and let Aelf address the Mountain Folk. "I want a small party of men and women to go with us to the cave where they are held. Too many people, and we will be discovered; not enough people, and we run the risk of leaving children behind."

The words were no sooner out of his mouth than the council area erupted in shouts. Men and women both jumped to their feet and began talking all at the same time. Aelf raised his hands for quiet, and Maeve rapped her staff repeatedly on the ground, but the Folk were overwhelmed with feelings and could not stop.

Suddenly a clear voice rang out from the back of the room, "Enough! Enough! Stop!" Conor's voice held a level of authority that the Folk recognized immediately.

They turned to look at the young boy who stood so straight and tall, his dog at his side, fists clenched and face white. "Sit down!" he commanded, and they obeyed. "This is Tilly we're talking about. This is Neall and Brian and Kevin we're talking about. These are our children, who have been missing longer than we want to think about. This is a force that we don't know anything about, but we have to figure out how to battle it and win them back. We can't just holler and shout. If we don't have a good plan, if we don't know everything we need to know and how to do exactly as we need to do it, we run the risk of failure. Of failing to bring our children home. We don't have time to argue. This is why we have leaders. Let them make the decisions that need to be made; let them lead us the way we've trusted them to do. When they are ready, they will tell us what we need to do, and we will do it!"

With that, Conor sat back down next to Cormac, who patted him on his back and whispered, "Well said, Conor!"

Erik Tamen watched all of this from the back of the room. He shook his head in wonder when Conor sat down. *Where did that boy get such strength? And why is it that all these Folk listened to him, a mere boy—a lowlander, at that?* Frankly puzzled, he watched Conor sit ramrod straight on his bench, eyes forward, waiting to hear what the council had to say.

Maeve rapped her stick once more. "We will meet as a council without the Folk to interrupt us. We will convene once more when a plan has been made. Then we will inform you all equally. Now go, please. Go home and let us work this out. Please."

The Mountain Folk slowly filed out, touching Conor on the shoulder or on his back as they left. Many mumbled an apology as they walked past him; many shook their heads as if to say how silly their neighbors were, but of course, they were much smarter and would wait until the council had it all worked out. Conor had their support, really, he did!

The council stood as one when the Folk had finished filing out. Maeve put her staff down and turned to face Granny. "Let us go to Aelf's dwelling, where we can sit and drink some of Shaen's good tea. There we will listen to each other and create a plan with your help."

Conor got up and started out of the council area. Erik Tamen stopped him before he got too far. "Where do you think you're going?"

"I'll wait with the rest of the Folk until you've decided what to do."

"I don't think so, Conor. I think we need your good sense as well as anyone here. I saw how the Folk listened to you. In fact, we all listened. There's a reason for that."

Conor shrugged, but he followed Erik Tamen as he joined the council and the others. Once in Aelf's dwelling, Shaen busied herself making tea for everyone. Looking up to count the number of people crowded around her fire, she realized she lacked enough cups. She turned to ask Ronan to fetch some of hers but found Cormac's face instead.

He smiled. "She went to get more cups, Shaen."

Shaen smiled at her husband's brother. "Yes, of course she would have anticipated that there would be a need. You are a fortunate man, Cormac, to have won such as her."

Cormac nodded his agreement and settled down with the rest of the Folk and the lowlanders he now considered his friends.

When tea was poured and everyone was quiet, Aelf looked to Erik, who nodded at him solemnly. Aelf spoke from his seat, wishing this to be less formal than a council meeting. "I want to hear from Matilda first, I think. I don't doubt she has a plan up there in her head, and I would like to hear it."

Granny sipped her tea for a moment, not to keep them in suspense but to gather her thoughts before she spoke. "I went to the cave last night and learned what I had hoped to learn. First of all, without going into details, I watched the woman do two things. The first was to bring a child out of a deep slumber, but not really awake. It is as if the child sleepwalks. The child can hear her commands and obey them, but there is no other awareness of speech or movement. The child is under the control of Ceobhran. The woman has learned the ancient words that control this creature. It is not a living creature, but rather like the wind or the mist that rises in the early morning. She is able to control it with her words. She sends it down to the valley and into the Mountain Folk village to steal our children. When Ceobhran touches you, you become it and it becomes you in an ancient way. As long as Ceobhran holds you, she can control you the same way she controls it.

"But there are other words she spoke. She had need of someone to follow the first child she sent out. Someone who could make decisions as well as follow her commands. In order to do that, this child needed to be fully awake, and so she used different words to release him from Ceobhran's grip. I heard these words as clearly as you hear my words now. I believe I can release the children, first from their deep sleep and then from the grip of Ceobhran. I am not sure, but I saw that the woman strokes the children and breathes upon them three times before she utters the words that wake them. I am not sure if that is necessary, but I am not willing to take the chance that I don't do everything she did."

Granny stopped to sip more tea. Looking around, she saw that all eyes were on her except for Conor's. His eyes were fixed on the floor, perhaps to keep the tears that gathered there from being noticed. No one spoke to ask a question or challenge Granny. They waited patiently for her to continue, most holding forgotten cups of tea.

"I know you all want to be part of this, but I am afraid for too many of us to go. Three times I have gone, and all three times, I have been discovered. I do not know how, because I know how to make myself small and insignificant, but still, they discover that I am there. Too many of us will only make it worse. I can only hope to sneak in and begin releasing children while someone else guides them out of the cave. If you are there, you can get the children to safety as quickly as possible. Enough distance between them and the woman might be all it takes to get them safely away."

Once again, voices were raised with questions. *"How will you be able to wake all of the children before you are discovered? How will you get away if they find you? What if they call up this Ceobhran and it takes all of us? Don't you think we should rush in and overtake them? There are only two of them, and many of us!"*

Granny shook her head, but before she could answer their questions, Erik spoke out. "Yes, there are many of us, but that might not be the difference we need. What we do need is something to distract them while Granny wakes the children. As I see it, I could do that. I could go into the cave before Granny does and pretend to be lost. With enough fast-talking, I could give her the chance to get as many out as possible."

No one spoke as they considered Erik's suggestion. Finally, Aelf spoke for them all. "I don't like it, Erik. None of us do, but it seems like the best way to get Matilda in and out without being noticed. What do you say, Matilda?"

Granny leveled her look at Erik and frowned, but try as she might, she couldn't come up with an argument. She knew that discovery was inevitable, and while she had no desire to throw her life away, she knew that it wasn't her life that was important but the lives of the children. "I agree," was all she said.

"Good, then it's settled. Now how many of us go?"

Cormac spoke up, as did Ronan. Shaen would not be denied a

chance to save her three boys. Maeve, though older, was no older than Granny. If she could do it, then so could Maeve. Conor spoke softly, "Wolf and I will go as well." Everyone nodded.

It was agreed, then, that the party of eight and one dog would leave at the first sign of morning sun. Morning meal would be eaten in the dark, food enough for four days would be packed, waterskins would be filled, and weapons would be assembled. Everyone would carry something along the way. Granny figured the better part of two days to reach the cave, though in truth, she had only traveled there in her mind, never by foot. They all agreed that Maeve and the rest of the council members would call a meeting and inform the Mountain Folk, but this time, there would be no discussion, only assent. They left Aelf's cave with plans to meet in the morning.

That evening as Granny and Conor packed, Conor said softly, "I don't much like this plan, Granny. It feels like too many people putting their lives in danger. I wish there was another way."

She smiled at him. "It makes as much sense as anything I've been able to come up with, Conor. You remember your promise to me? To stay outside and help the children escape?"

Conor shook his head but did not argue with her. "I'm going to take my bow and the arrows that Cormac helped me make. I haven't had too much of a chance to practice with them, but I will feel better having a weapon of any kind. I don't know how much sleep we'll get, but I will see you in the morning."

25

FINDING SEAN

The sky showed the faintest blush of color from the rising sun when they gathered outside Aelf's cave. Erik had on a pair of hide moccasins from the Mountain Folk and carried a new staff to replace his lost one. Ronan was wrapped in her cloak to keep away the morning chill, a heavy pack slung over one shoulder. Cormac carried his bow and a quiver of arrows fletched with new feathers over one shoulder and his pack over the other. Maeve wore a heavy cloak and carried her staff and a small pack. Conor waited patiently, bow, arrows, and pack slung over his shoulder and Wolf at his side. Granny gripped her wool skirt with one hand while the other held her pack in place.

Aelf and Shaen came out of their doorway with packs and walking sticks. "I can do more damage with a walking stick than most people can do with any other weapon," growled Aelf. Cormac smiled at his brother in agreement. He had seen firsthand the lethal weapon that a stout stick became in Aelf's hands, though he preferred the distance that his bow and arrows offered him when confronted. "We are ready. Let us go now!"

As the hunter who had explored every inch of the mountains and valleys between, Aelf led the way, with the rest walking single file and

Erik Tamen in the rear. It was a quiet group of people that morning that wound their way through the forest, finding the game trails that carried them higher and higher. Lost in their thoughts, no words necessary. Some wondered if they would see their homes again, some dreamed of holding their children, and some marveled that the fates had brought them together, such an odd group of people.

Granny mumbled the ancient words over and over to herself while she walked. She thought of Tilly and wondered if she had returned from the valley where Mara had sent her. She thought about the young boy that Mara had sent after her. *Why did he call her 'Mother'? Do all the children think of Mara that way, or is there a connection between the two?* She shook her head. It didn't matter. What mattered was that Conor stay outside. Mara must not be allowed to see him. Nor did she want Conor to see the woman. *Please, if I could just do this thing, then I could leave this world satisfied.*

Aelf set a fast pace and did not ask if they needed to rest. Determined to put as much distance behind them as possible before nightfall overtook them, he ordered them to drink their water as they walked. He would give them a rest at midday and allow time for a short meal. There was a deep gorge that he had in mind for spending the night, and there was no time to waste getting there. The trees had shed the leaves that were renewed each year. The crunch of the dry leaves under their feet announced their passage. Nearby, deer threw up their heads and sniffed the air. The scent of man reached their noses, and they bounded off to safety. Birds flew up from the trees to whirl overhead before flying off to warn the forest that man was coming. A lone black bear stood on his back feet and raised his head. His nose crinkled at the smell, and his sharp ears told him what his eyes could not; men passed this way, and it was time to leave.

Midday found them in a copse of alder trees, underneath naked branches spread across the sky. Aelf spread his cloak on the ground, and he and Shaen sat together to eat. The others, too tired to eat, sat silently, leaning against tree trunks and closing their eyes. "If you don't eat now, you won't eat until nightfall," Aelf growled.

Obediently, they opened their packs and took out meat and bread wrapped in cloth. Shaen passed out the delicious cakes she'd made from ground nuts and dried fruit cooked in bear fat. The fat would give them much-needed energy for the rest of the day. Water skins were raised, and the cool water trickled down throats parched and dry.

"There should be a stream up ahead just a ways. The fates allowing, there is still water this time of the year, and we can fill our skins. To be safe, save some of your water."

Midday meal was short, and Aelf had them back on their feet and marching once more. Despite the fast pace, the steady uphill climb, and the lack of rest, no one complained. Although weary, each was determined not to be the first to give in to their aching bodies and tired feet.

It was halfway through the afternoon when Aelf suddenly raised his right hand to call a halt. Maeve leaned against her staff to rest, while the others looked to see what Aelf was seeing in the distance. The path led them down a small incline before rising again to climb. Down at the bottom, they could clearly see a small pillar of smoke rising into the air above. Aelf stood and puzzled for a moment. "That's odd," he said. "I have no trackers out in this part of the mountains. Who but us would be out here at this time of the year? That is our path, and we must take it, but keep an eye out for anything that looks out of place."

Once again, they formed their line and followed him down the path toward the bottom of the incline. He stopped some distance from the smoke, and now they could clearly smell it. No scent of roasting meat, just of the smoke. "Stay here," he ordered and moved forward.

They were more than happy to sit and wait, taking this chance to rest. Erik and Conor both stayed on their feet, one looking up the path, the other down the way that Aelf had gone. Soon enough, they heard him call out to them, "Come in, all is good."

They gathered up their packs, walking sticks, and weapons and followed him to the smoke. There, huddled near the small fire, was the shape of a thin man with wild, unkempt hair and ragged clothes.

He looked up in surprise as the group approached, but then a smile split his face in two, and his eyes lit up like a child's on Beltane morn.

Granny gasped when she saw the poor figure huddled around his fire. "Sean, what in goodness are you doing out here?"

Erik Tamen pushed through the line to see what Granny was talking about. "Sean, is that you? What are you doing out here, man?" Disbelief crossed his face as he looked at the disheveled figure on the ground before the fire.

Sean struggled to his feet, brushing off his clothes and running fingers through his hair. He squared his shoulders and looked Erik in the eye. "Why, I've come looking for you, Erik. I've come to help bring our children home. That's what I'm doing. I'm just not doing a real fine job of it, is all."

Ronan reached Sean first. "You poor, poor man. When was the last time you ate?" She began taking food out of her pack and pressing it into his hands.

For just a moment, Sean stared at his hands and the food in them, blinking. He raised them to his nose and breathed deeply, inhaling the rich smell of meat, roasted with herbs and rubbed with fat. He looked at Ronan with tears in his eyes and offered it back to her. "I can't take this," he said. "I have nothing but water to offer you."

She smiled at him and pushed his hands away. "I will gladly take your water, for I drank all of mine and was worried that I would die of thirst before this day was over."

With tears streaming down his face, Sean chewed the meat and accepted the cakes she gave him next. They all gathered around Sean and pressed more food into his hands: cheese made from goat milk, dried berries and nuts, strips of deer and bear meat, until he held up his hands in protest. "I swear I have no room for another bite!"

Erik Tamen sat across from him. "Now tell us, Sean, how are you here? How long have you been up in these mountains? Where is your food? What in all the name of the fates are you doing here by yourself?"

"I came to find you, to help if I could. I will be honest, Erik. It was not entirely my idea. The villagers helped me make up my mind to come. I did not do a good job of running the village after you left. I made mistakes, and I made everyone angry. Doireann packed me food, but only enough for one meal. I found some wild onions and grains that I cooked, but I haven't had any of that for days now. I found a good piece of flint so that I could build a fire to keep me warm and safe from animals, but I was afraid to go any farther. I am glad now that I kept my fire going. I think that is how you found me?"

Aelf nodded. "We saw your smoke from above. You are lucky that we came this way. I don't know if you would have lasted much longer."

Sean shook his head. "I think you are right. I was prepared to die here, but instead, I am in the company of good people, and I have food in my belly. Now, if only I had a pinch of tobacco for my pipe, my world would be complete."

Cormac laughed and dug into his pack. "That I can help you with. I grow enough tobacco to fill every pipe in my village. I am happy to share some."

Once again, tears of joy coursed down Sean's face, and he pulled his pipe out of his pocket and passed it to Cormac to fill. He took a small stick from the edge of the fire and held it to his pipe to light it. With his eyes closed, he blew the smoke out and smiled. "That is good tobacco, my friend. Thank you! Now, if someone would explain to me who you all are, I would be happy to listen."

Granny laughed. "I guess we do make a strange sight here. Sean, Conor and I left to find Erik, who had been injured on his travels through the mountains. These are Mountain Folk, and they found Erik and took him in. We have been living with them, waiting for Erik to recover. Aelf is their leader; Shaen is his wife. This is Cormac, his brother; Ronan, their healer; and Maeve, the head of their council. We know where the children are, and we travel now to bring them home. It has taken far longer than we hoped, but there were reasons for the delay. I think perhaps you should stay here by your fire, and we will come and find you when the children are safe."

Sean struggled to his feet and faced Granny with a fierce scowl. "No! I have come this far, and I do not mean to sit on the side any longer. Granny, please. Listen to me. I have been in this forest and these mountains for more days than I can remember, but I never gave up. For once in my life, I want to see something through. Please don't ask me to stay behind. You might walk off and leave me, but I will follow you. I have to, don't you see? I have let everyone down, over and over. Myself, mostly. I don't want to do that any longer." Voice filled with passion, Sean pleaded with them all.

Aelf exchanged glances with Erik Tamen, who shrugged his shoulders. "You will have to keep up. We have no time to wait for anyone who cannot keep up."

Sean gathered up his stick, his meager pack, and his cloak. He kicked dirt on his fire to put it out and squared his shoulders. "I am ready," he declared.

By nightfall, they began the climb down into the gorge where Aelf had proposed they spend the night. They built a fire with the help of Sean's flint and shared their meal together. Too tired to talk, they ate in silence and, wrapping themselves in their cloaks, fell asleep under trees and shrubs.

Morning found Maeve stirring the remnants of their fire and heating water for tea. Aelf grumbled at the delay. His plan was to chew some dried meat as they walked, but for once he gave in to Maeve's direct stare when he questioned her.

"This just might be the last meal I have on this good earth, Aelf. I plan on sitting to eat it and drinking some tea like a human being."

Granny chuckled to herself. She did like a woman with a bit of bite in her!

Midday found them at the bottom of the last mountain, the one with dark clouds that swirled around and around its peak but never drifted off in the sky. Aelf found a game trail that wound back and forth in a switchback, taking an indirect path to reach the highest peak. The group rested once more, ate a cold meal of cheese and bread, and talked about their plan.

"I want Ronan to come in with me when I wake the children." Granny kept her eyes on the group as she spoke. "She knows the ancient words and the touch. Two of us waking the children will be much faster than one. We will go in first and hide ourselves. Beyond the main part of the cave is a passageway to a back chamber. Erik will come in after us and make his way to the back of the cave, where he will make a good deal of noise and commotion. The point is to keep the man and woman busy with him in the back chamber so that Ronan and I can work. The passageway is narrow and long with twists and turns, and I think that will help us hide from their view. I worry that Erik will not be able to get away, but if he is convincing enough, they might not suspect him of anything. We will place the cloth back over the sleeping platforms, so at a quick glance, it will seem as if the children are still there."

Granny continued, "Once they are awake, we will send them outside, and when you have a small group of them, hurry them down the path and away from the cave. One of you stay there with the children, and the others come back for more. Keep this up until we all come out together. Agreed? It is not the best plan, but it is the only plan we have right now."

Everyone nodded their agreement. Sean looked back and forth between the group. "You mean to tell me that a man and woman stole our children and have them hidden in a cave? How do you know all this, Granny?"

"Please trust me, Sean. You have asked us to trust you and allow you to come with us. Now it is your turn to trust us. I will answer your questions once we are off this cursed mountain, but for now I need to rest and gather my strength."

No one questioned Granny's words. "It is settled then. If everyone knows what it is they are responsible for, I say we get this over with and bring these children home."

As a group, they rose and gathered up their belongings. Cormac and Conor held their bows in their hands, each notched with an arrow. The others had determined looks on their faces as they followed Aelf upward.

26

THE CHILDREN

G ranny left the main part of the group a few hundred paces from the entrance to the cave. She and Ronan crept forward, with Erik some steps behind them. They hesitated at the entrance to the cave, felt the cold, stale air wash over them, and gripped each other's hands. Letting go first, Granny moved forward on cat's feet, mindful of the loose sand under her shoes. She gripped her wool skirt with both hands to keep them still and bent over as if to make herself even smaller than she was. Ronan imitated her walk, doubling her body into a smaller package. They made their way to the side wall and there, huddled against it in the dark, allowed time for their eyes to adjust. Not daring to breathe, they commanded their hearts to still so that even that sound was silenced. Here, they waited for a bumbling Erik Tamen to wander into the cave as if lost.

Erik stood at the entrance and took a deep breath. He thought longingly of his dear Guin waiting for him at home. Would he see her again? Would he be himself after this day, or would he be as the children were, forever asleep and held by a monster he could not see? More than anything, he wanted to run away from this place, wake up in bed with the sun streaming through the window and Guin cooking breakfast. He wanted to walk through his beloved village, tell his jokes and stories, laugh with the villagers, and be at home once more. He marveled at the turn of events that had brought him to this point, brought all of them to this point. He wondered if the children would wake up; would they be willing to obey Granny and Ronan, would they ever be safe? He waited until he was sure that Granny and Ronan were well hidden, and then he stumbled into the cave.

Walking past the sleeping platforms, he made his way toward a light at the back of the chamber, which seemed to go on forever. Once near the passageway, he began to call out, "Is there anyone here? Is there anyone about? I am lost, and I need some help!"

Almost immediately, he heard voices from the back of the passageway, and soon a disheveled man with a thick, black beard and straggly hair that brushed his shoulders came cautiously forward, holding a lighted branch. Erik frowned when he saw the man. There was something familiar about him, but he couldn't quite place it. Had he seen this man somewhere before?

Jebez stopped and held up the light to see Erik better. "What are you doing here? You are not allowed in here!"

Erik shook his head as if puzzled. "I am sorry. I don't mean to intrude, but the truth is, I am lost up here in these blasted mountains. I saw your cave and thought it might be a good place to spend the night. Am I ever happy to see your fire and find you here. I thought I was going to die up here. Come on, let's go sit by your fire." Erik grabbed his arm and began dragging him toward the light.

Jebez tried in vain to shake off his grip, but Erik had all his oak-like strength behind that grip, and Jebez was powerless to escape it. Erik dragged him farther down the passageway, all the while exclaiming how lucky he was to have found someone here in these godforsaken mountains.

Granny gestured to Ronan, and they slipped together from the wall. Granny quickly scurried on slippered feet to the far side of the chamber, where she pulled back the first cloth that she came to. "*Eirich, eirich e cogar, ogfhear.* Arise, arise and listen, boy." She stroked the boy's face and brushed the hair from his forehead as she spoke. The boy sat up and swung his feet over the platform. He stared straight ahead with no expression. Granny stroked his face once more, breathing into his face, muttering the words as she did, "*Ackman, Ceobhran. Ackman!* Release him, Ceobhran. Release him!"

The boy blinked and looked around him. He turned his head and looked at Granny with a face full of questions. She grabbed him by the hand and dragged him off the platform, steering him toward the entrance to the cave. "Go! Run! There are good people out there who are waiting for you. Now go!" The boy looked once more at Granny and then did as she commanded, running as fast as his feet could carry him toward the entrance.

Granny immediately turned to the next platform, where the cloth revealed the one she hoped to find, Tilly! Touching her sweet face, she spoke the words that brought her to a seated position, "*Eirich, eirich e cogar, ainmhi baineann!*" Tilly's face was blank and her eyes dark, with no light behind them. Granny quickly smoothed her face, breathed on her, and spoke again, "*Ackman, ackman, Ceobhran!*"

Tilly shuddered as if a cold wind had blown over her body. She blinked and shuddered once more. Granny wrapped her thin arms around the girl and held her tight. "Oh, Granny, is that you? Oh, Granny, I hurt all over!" she cried.

Granny took her arms away and pressed her finger to Tilly's lips. She leaned in close to Tilly's ear and whispered, "I need your help. I am going to try to awaken the children, and I need you to take them out of this wretched cave. Can you do that, Tilly? Are you able?"

Tilly nodded and did not speak again. Granny slipped to the next sleeping form and repeated her actions. Once the child was fully awake, Tilly grabbed her hand and pulled her toward the light outside. Once outside, she looked in amazement at the people there, people she did not recognize until one form left the group and came hurtling toward her, nearly knocking her off her feet. Wolf was joined by a young boy with a shock of brown hair that fell across his forehead and a smile that split his face in two. Grabbing her and holding her close, Conor shook with the sobs that racked him. At length, he pushed off and held her at arm's length. Her face was white and her eyes wide with wonder. "I don't understand, Conor. I don't understand!"

"Where is Granny?" His voice was strained.

"I have to go back. I am supposed to bring the children out to you. Please wait for me, Conor."

She whirled and ran back into the cave in time to gather another child from Granny and one from Ronan. Taking both children by the hand, she led them out to join the others. She looked longingly at Conor, who took the children from her, but there was no time for words. She knew without being told that time was working against them.

Erik released his grip and slung his arm over Jebez's shoulder, proclaiming loudly how lucky he was to find a friend so far from home. As they made their way to the back of the cave, Mara quickly spread a bundle of cloth over the heaps of silver bowls and candle-sticks on the floor of the cave, hiding everything from the view of this nosy stranger.

"Jebez, what do you have here?" she queried sweetly.

"My dear, a stranger wandered into our cave. He's lost, he says."

Jebez? Erik's eyes widened. *Is this the same Jebez who wandered like a gypsy into our town and stayed for years? Is this the same Jebez that left in the middle of the night, leaving a small boy behind?* Erik ducked his head to hide the look of surprise on his face.

Mara held out her hands in welcome. *No sense arousing his suspicion,* she thought. "Welcome, welcome. We are only here as a retreat from the madness of the world. We thought if we could spend some time here in this cave, alone with just each other, we might find comfort in our solitude. You are welcome to share just a bit of it with us, and then Jebez will help you find your way down the mountain to wherever you are going. Meanwhile, tell me where you come from."

Erik took his hand from Jebez's shoulder and sat down on a ledge at the far side of the chamber. He shrugged. "I am from everywhere and nowhere," he said. "I travel, mostly. I thought to see what was on the other side of the mountain." He chuckled. "I thought I was a better tracker than I am, so here I am, lost as a goose. If I could trouble you for a cup of tea, that would suit me. Then I will be on my way."

Mara's eyes narrowed as she stared at Erik. There was something about this man that bothered her. There was a feeling that she knew him from somewhere, but where? She gestured to Jebez to fix tea for them all and continued to watch Erik. Erik let his eyes wander around the ceiling of the cave, pretending an interest in it. He hoped to avoid her eyes if at all possible.

Jebez brought tea and handed a cup to Erik, who blew on it to cool it. Mara's eyes narrowed further. She had seen that look somewhere. Where?

Granny and Ronan scurried from platform to platform while Tilly gathered up the waking children and hurried them out of the cave. Maeve took the first group to a clearing about halfway down the mountain and sat with them, holding their hands and murmuring soft words to them. Aelf and Cormac shuffled the children in pairs down to Maeve, who kept them quiet and safe. Sean, still weak from his days without food, stayed outside the cave to help calm the frightened children. You could not drag Conor away from the cave entrance, where he waited for another and another glimpse of Tilly as she rushed out with more children. Every time she turned to go back in, Conor felt his heart give a jerk and his breath catch in his throat. He wanted nothing more than to rush back in with her and help ferry the children to safety, but mindful of the promise that he made to Granny, he stayed outside.

"You say you are a traveler, friend? Where do you travel to? Are you a tinker selling wares, because I see nothing about you that indicates you have much to sell?" Mara questioned Erik as he sat drinking the tea that Jebez brewed.

"No, I don't sell anything. I might stay a while in a town or village, working in a blacksmith shop or hauling freight, but when I'm tired of the town, I move on to the next one. I've seen a lot of the world, let me tell you." Erik knew it was just a matter of time before Mara recognized him. He was confident that Jebez would never remember him from the village, but he had had more dealings with Mara. He watched her narrow her eyes in thought as she stared at him. He kept his head ducked low to avoid her eyes and mumbled his answers through his beard. How long would it take Granny and Ronan to retrieve the children? That was one part of the plan they hadn't thought out.

Now is not a good time to remember that, he thought. *I can't keep sitting here forever. Once I finish this blasted tea, I am going to have to leave. What if they aren't finished? We can't leave children behind.* Erik did not get to finish that thought, because Mara suddenly raised her head and looked him squarely in the face.

"You! I do know you! You . . . you are from that wretched little village in the valley. You are not a traveler. You . . . yes, you were the mayor! This is not an accident that you are here! Jebez, hold him!"

Jebez dropped his cup of tea, scalding his leg. He jumped up in pain, only to have Erik's fist catch him on the chin and knock him backward. Erik didn't wait for Mara's reaction. He turned and ran down the passageway, hoping to reach it and warn Granny before Mara could follow.

Granny and Ronan had the last of the children awake. The many cloths were draped over the sleeping platforms to hide their emptiness. Tilly had taken the last two hands in hers and started toward the entrance, when Erik burst through the passageway into the chamber. Tilly turned back in confusion. "Erik?"

Granny yelled, "Go, Tilly. Take the children out now!" She stood and faced the passageway that she knew would bring Mara and Jebez. Erik skidded to a stop near her, and Ronan rushed to join them both. They faced what they knew was coming together.

Tilly grabbed the two children and ran for the outside. "They're in trouble," she gasped. "I don't know what's going on, but Erik Tamen just ran from the back of the cave as if his life depended on it. Granny told me to run with the last of the children. But, Conor, I'm afraid for her. I'm afraid for them all!"

Conor took her arms in his hands. "Listen to me, Tilly. Take these last two down the path. You'll find some people down there that you don't know, but trust them, because I do. They have the children safely there. Go, Tilly. I will see you when I get Granny out."

He gave Tilly a push and turned back to the cave.

Mara entered the chamber and stopped dead. "I should have known, you crazy old woman. I should have known that you would be back. I just didn't know you were mad enough to bring friends."

Granny stepped forward, and as she did, she hissed to Erik and Ronan, "Back out as quickly as you can. Don't turn your back on her, but back out now!" She took another step toward Mara and waved her hand behind her to motion the two of them away.

Ronan looked uncertainly at Erik, who grimaced and took a step forward.

"Back, I said! Back," Granny hissed once more.

Ronan reached out and grabbed Erik's arm and tugged as hard as she could on the mountain of a man.

Mara walked confidently toward Granny, and as she did, she held out her hand and spread her fingers. Granny stiffened in place but did not move. Slowly, she raised her hand and held it in front of her, the palm facing Mara. Mara's eyes widened in surprise, and she stopped still. "Oh, you have power I did not know you had, old woman. You might be able to stop me, but you cannot stop Ceobhran."

What happened next happened so quickly that no one's account seemed to match when they recounted it later. Mara threw back her head and screamed, "*Ceobhran, tar ar ais. Tar ar ais e cabhru! Geilleadh, Ceobrahn, geilleadh!*"

Immediately, a mist began to rise from the floor of the cave, swirling until it formed a shape that held together. Mara continued to scream the strange words, which echoed throughout the chamber.

Jebez ran in and stood behind her, looking with satisfaction at the three rescuers. *Now they'll see what power Mara has*, he thought. *Now we will see who wins this battle!*

Granny continued to hold her hand against the will of Mara, despite the shaking that overtook it. She raised her voice over her shoulder, "Run! Erik, Ronan, run!"

Ronan grabbed Erik's hand once more, and though he was still as stout as ever, her fright gave her strength she never knew she had. Tugging him backward, she never took her eyes off Granny and the mist that had begun to make its way inexorably toward the woman.

Sean and Conor heard the uproar from outside, and despite promises made, they both rushed into the cave. The sight froze them in their tracks. Mara with her head thrown back and her throat stretched tight, screaming words that were incomprehensible to them. Jebez standing behind her, with a maniacal look of joy on his face. Granny with arm outstretched, shaking so badly that it appeared it might fly off her shoulder. Ronan pulling on Erik's hand, dragging him backward.

Sean gasped. "Mara? Jebez? You . . . you're here? You . . . you are the cause of all of this? You are the cause of all this misery?" Sean took a step forward and raised his hand to point at Mara. His voice echoed throughout the cave.

Conor took in the scene with confusion written on his face, and then something in Sean's voice made him start. *What did the man say? Does he know these people?* Confusion flooded his face as he looked from Sean to the screaming woman and the man behind her. A sort of deadness came over him as he looked at them. No! It couldn't be. It was impossible! Yet there it was. The woman and the man that he remembered, not from memories but from dreams he had had all his life. Dreams of this man and woman, who left him behind as if he were of no consequence to them.

Ronan succeeded in dragging Erik back to where Sean gaped at Mara and Jebez. The mist, holding together more solidly now, made its way toward Granny. She felt it coming, but all her power right now was being used to hold the two back. She had nothing left to hold back the mist.

Sean moved forward, and just as the tendrils of mist reached out to gather Granny in its embrace, he pushed her aside and leaped toward Mara. A growl rose from his throat, his hands reached for her neck, and wrapping his fingers around it, he began to shake her, whipping her long black hair from side to side. "You witch! You killed my mother! You stole my life!" His anguished voice rose to the top of the cave and reverberated through the dim light.

The mist crept across the floor, reaching Sean, and together, he and Mara fell to the ground. The mist fanned out and covered them completely in a soft blanket of white. Their forms on the cave floor softened and lay still as the mist thickened and swallowed them.

Granny dropped her arm and whirled to flee as fast as her feet could move. She pushed the others in front of her, and together they ran from the cave. "Don't stop! Just run!" Tripping and falling, somehow the four of them managed to get down the path to the clearing below.

When they burst into the clearing, Tilly jumped to her feet and ran to Conor. He held her tightly and would not let her go. Granny sat on a log and put her arm around Ronan's shoulders. "We did it," she whispered. "We did it!"

27

GOING HOME

Conor stared at Granny from across the clearing, his face like stone. She met his gaze and nodded her head. Yes, she was guilty of keeping things from him, but she didn't regret it, and if it had not gone the way it did, she would have kept this secret to her grave.

"Where's Sean?" asked Maeve. "I don't see him."

"He won't be coming," Erik answered wearily. "He stayed behind."

Maeve looked puzzled, but for now their job was to get the children out of the mountains safely. Gathering them up, they started down the path.

"We should have brought more food," muttered Cormac. "How are we going to feed these children?"

Ronan took his hand and smiled. "My good, practical Cormac. I guess we'll share the little we have and feed them up right when we get home."

Aelf and Shaen walked with their three boys between them, alternately crying and laughing. Their behavior confused the boys, especially the tears shed by their father, a man not known for his tender emotions. After a while, they shrugged and went along with it, happy to be outside in the sunshine.

Tilly walked beside Conor, resting her head on his shoulder

when she could. Wolf danced around the two of them, giving Tilly a quick flicker-kiss of the tongue, then Conor.

Granny walked with Erik, and they spoke softly. "You gave us the time we needed to get the children away. Thank you, Erik."

"Did you know all this time that it was Mara and Jebez?" Erik asked.

"Yes, but I couldn't say it for fear that Conor would hear. I didn't tell you because I was afraid that you would give yourself away. I gambled that you wouldn't recognize them, or they you. I gambled, and I lost!"

"I'd say you won, Granny Matilda. I'd say we all won, even Sean, in a way."

Granny looked at him oddly, but frankly was too tired to question him further.

It took two full days to bring the children back to the Mountain Folk village. Once there, the children were fed and fussed over. The Mountain Folk marveled at all the children, not just their children, and wondered how they would all find their way back home. A meeting of the council was called, first to thank the group of eight brave souls who had risked everything to bring the children out safely. Then the discussion turned to the problem of returning the children to their homes. After much discussion, it was decided that the Mountain Folk should leave the mountains and help the children home once more. There was fear in this decision, fear that going to the valley would end in disaster, but in the end, the Folk all agreed it was the right thing to do. Ronan volunteered to take the first group down to the valley, and Cormac quickly offered to join her.

Conor spent a lot of time alone with Wolf, shunning even Tilly, for once in his life. Cormac sought him out finally and sat with him. "Tell me, Conor. Your heart is troubled, and I don't understand why. You have Tilly home, Granny is safe, and you will soon be going back to your village. Is Sean's death weighing on you, son?"

Conor shook his head. "I am sad about Sean, but that's not what's hurting me. Those people, Cormac, the ones who did this . . . they are my parents! My parents, and I never knew it. Granny never told me!

How am I supposed to live with that? How can I face the villagers knowing that it was my parents, Mara and Jebez who did this to them?"

Cormac was silent for long minutes. Finally, he said, "What an enormous burden to carry, Conor."

"I know. How am I supposed to live with the knowledge that my parents did this?"

"You misunderstand me, son. I don't mean this is your burden to carry. You are not responsible for the actions of others. You know that the Mountain Folk long ago learned that we only carry the responsibility of our own actions, not those of others. I am talking about the burden that Granny carried. She knew how much this would hurt you, and she tried to do everything in her power to protect you from the knowledge. I wondered when I saw her glare at Ronan when she almost said the woman's name. I wondered why she never told anyone. It was to protect you, son. It is a terrible burden to know that you carry something that has the power to hurt someone you love. I hope that someday you are grown enough to understand this and forgive her." Cormac rose and patted Conor on the back.

Wolf sat with Conor for a long time, looking out into the woods that surrounded them. Together they saw a deer walk hesitantly forward to find the last of the sweet grass that grew in the sunshine. Wolf started as though to give chase, but Conor rested his hand on the dog's head. "Let it go, Wolf. Let it go." He stood and stretched his arms to the sky. "Let's go back, Wolf. I think it's time I took my own advice and let it go."

The mountain stood cold and dark in the last of the evening light, black clouds swirling around and around its peaks, constantly moving but never blowing away. There, in the back of a cave so deep and dark that no light entered, a man fussed over two forms, each sleeping on a rock platform. He pulled the cloth back from one of the shapes and, using a brush made of hog's bristles, began to untangle the mass of black hair the color of a raven's wing. Gently and with love, he brushed and brushed the long black hair, humming an ancient tune as he did.

The End

www.ingramcontent.com/pod-product-compliance
Lightning Source LLC
Chambersburg PA
CBHW070024120726
47909CB00003B/1055